W9-ASJ-418

PENGUIN CLASSICS

THE STORY OF HONG GILDONG

MINSOO KANG is an associate professor of history at the University of Missouri–St. Louis, specializing in the cultural and intellectual history of Western Europe in the eighteenth and nineteenth centuries. In addition to articles in numerous journals, he is the author of *Sublime Dreams of Living Machines: The Automaton in the European Imagination* and the coeditor of *Visions of the Industrial Age, 1830–1914: Modernity and the Anxiety of Representation in Europe.* He is also a fiction writer and has published the short story collection *Of Tales and Enigmas.*

The Story of Hong Gildong

Translated with an Introduction and Notes by
MINSOO KANG

4528 6925
East Baton Rouge Parish Library
Baton Rouge, Louisiana

PENGUIN BOOKS

PENGUIN BOOKS

An imprint of Penguin Random House LLC
375 Hudson Street
New York, New York 10014
penguin.com

This translation, in different form, appeared in *Azalea: A Journal of Korean Literature and Culture*, vol. 6 (Cambridge, MA: Harvard University Korean Institute), 2013.

The Story of Hong Gildong is published with the support of the
Literature Translation Institute of Korea (LTI Korea).

Translation, introduction, and notes copyright © 2016 by Minsoo Kang
Penguin supports copyright. Copyright fuels creativity, encourages diverse voices, promotes free speech, and creates a vibrant culture. Thank you for buying an authorized edition of this book and for complying with copyright laws by not reproducing, scanning, or distributing any part of it in any form without permission. You are supporting writers and allowing Penguin to continue to publish books for every reader.

LIBRARY OF CONGRESS CATALOGING-IN-PUBLICATION DATA
Ho, Kyun, 1569–1618.
[Hong Kil-tong chon. English]
The story of Hong Gildong / translated with an introduction and Notes by Minsoo Kang.
pages cm—(Penguin classics)
Includes bibliographical references.
ISBN 978-0-14-310769-9
I. Kang, Minsoo, translator. II. Title.
PL989.27.K9H613 2016
895.13'46—dc23
2015018815

Printed in the United States of America
1 3 5 7 9 10 8 6 4 2

This translation is dedicated to the memory of Michael Henry Heim (1943–2012), a truly great translator whom I had the privilege of knowing as a man of remarkable wisdom and kindness.

Contents

Introduction

The Story of Hong Gildong is arguably the single most important work of classic (i.e., premodern) prose fiction of Korea, in terms not only of its literary achievement but also of its influence on the larger culture. In the modern era the iconic narrative has been retold, revised, and updated countless times in fiction, film, television shows, and comic books. Even Koreans who have never actually read the original work in full are familiar with the tale of the illegitimate son of a nobleman and his lowborn concubine who leaves home in frustration at the treatment he receives from his family, becomes the leader of a band of outlaws who dedicate themselves to robbing the rich and the powerful, and finally leaves the country to become the king of his own realm. Most Koreans can recite the hero Hong Gildong's lament at his condition as an illegitimate child, that even though he is a sturdy man of great talent he is not allowed to "address his father as Father and his older brother as Brother."

A figure as quintessentially Korean as Robin Hood is English (one could mention other heroic outlaws like Song Jiang of China, Nezumi Kozō of Japan, Juro Jánošik of Slovakia, Salvatore Giuliano of Sicily, Ned Kelly of Australia, and Jesse James of Missouri[1]), the presence of Hong Gildong in Korean culture is ubiquitous even today. One apparent indication of this is the widespread use of his name as the generic cognomen in the manner of "John Doe." Instructions on how to fill out forms commonly use Hong Gildong to indicate where one's name should be written, and the English-language Wikipedia article "Korean Names" features an illustration with "Hong Gildong" in both the *hangeul* phonetic script (홍길동) and Chinese ideograms (洪吉童).[2]

Despite the importance of *The Story of Hong Gildong* to Korean literature and culture, scholarly study of the work has been hampered throughout the modern period by certain misconceptions about its origin and significance. Unfortunately, these misconceptions have been firmly established in the public consciousness through repetition in Korean school textbooks. The most prevalent of them are the following:

1. *Hong Gildong jeon* (*The Story of Hong Gildong*) was written by the Joseon dynasty[3] poet and statesman Heo Gyun (1569–1618).
2. *Hong Gildong jeon* is a narrative manifesto of Heo Gyun's radical political ideas.
3. *Hong Gildong jeon* is the first work of fiction to be originally composed in *hangeul*, the phonetic script invented by King Sejong the Great in the fifteenth century.

In modern scholarship, these ideas became widespread through the colonial-era literary scholar Kim Taejun's pioneering work, *History of Joseon Fiction* (*Joseon soseolsa*), which was first serialized in the newspaper *Donga ilbo* from 1930 to 1931, and then collected in book form in 1933. As the first full-length study of classic Korean fiction, it has exerted an enormous influence on all subsequent works on the subject. Many of the most influential texts on traditional Korean literature repeat most of Kim's ideas, sometimes verbatim. As a nationalist and a communist, Kim Taejun presented a subversive reading of *The Story of Hong Gildong*, in which he portrayed the purported author, Heo Gyun, as a protosocialist who planned a revolution to overthrow the kingdom in order to create a more egalitarian state in its place and wrote the work to criticize the feudalistic order of Joseon.[4] Recently, however, scholars have had to grapple with numerous mistakes, unsupported assertions, and ideological interpreta-tions in *History of Joseon Fiction* that have solidified into stan-dard readings.

The sole basis for the attribution of the work to Heo Gyun comes from the writings of Yi Sik (1584–1647), who was once a student of Heo but later turned against him for reasons of court politics. In a rather unflattering portrait of his former teacher, Yi claims that Heo and his closest friends were such admirers of the Chinese epic novel of heroic bandits *Water Margin* (*Shuihu-zhuan*) that he wrote *Hong Gildong jeon* in imitation.[5] Because Yi Sik emerged as one of the most important literary figures of his time, his assertion that Heo Gyun wrote a story about the his-torical bandit (there are a few records of an outlaw named Hong Gildong who was captured by the authorities in 1500) was re-peated numerous times by various writers. There is, however, no evidence that Yi Sik had seen such a work, and none that can demonstrate that the work ostensibly written by Heo Gyun in the seventeenth century is related in any way to *The Story of Hong Gildong* as we know it today. In fact, there is no record of anyone actually having read a work entitled *The Story of Hong Gildong* until the second half of the nineteenth century.

In a 2012 article, Lee Yoon Suk, an expert on classic Korean fiction, published his discovery that Kim Taejun was, in fact, not the first modern scholar to attribute *The Story of Hong Gildong* to Heo Gyun.[6] Given the importance of the work to Korean culture and identity, it is rather ironic that it was a Jap-anese scholar named Takahashi Toru (1878–1967), a professor of Joseon literature and Kim Taejun's teacher at Keijō Imperial University, who made the problematic attribution in 1927. Takahashi also made the further claim that Heo Gyun must have originally written it in Chinese characters since noble *yang-ban* writers like Heo eschewed the use of *hangeul*, which they referred to derogatorily as *eonmun* (vulgar script). The contrary but equally problematic notion that *The Story of Hong Gil-dong* was the first work of fiction to be composed in *hangeul* was not made until 1948 by Yi Myeongseon in his book *History of*

xii   INTRODUCTION

Joseon Literature (*Joseon munhaksa*).[7] While it appears to be the case that the work was first written in the phonetic script, neither Yi nor anyone else has provided any evidence that it was the first *hangeul* fiction.

The general view that *The Story of Hong Gildong* was written in the seventeenth century by Heo Gyun as a kind of literary manifesto of his radical politics is based on a series of historical and literary myths. An objective assessment of Heo Gyun's life reveals him to be an excellent literary scholar but a substandard government official and a political opportunist who was ultimately executed not for attempting to foment a revolution that would usher in an egalitarian state, but actually for running afoul of powerful figures in the royal court. It is unfortunately the case, however, that the attribution of the writing to him and the interpretation of the story as subversive of Joseon's feudal order remain the standard views of the work in Korean scholarship.

Recent research and reassessment of the history of Joseon dynasty literature have yielded a much more plausible picture of the origin of *The Story of Hong Gildong* and its historical context. Under the able leadership of the eighteenth-century monarchs Yeongjo (r. 1724–1776) and Jeongjo (r. 1776–1800), Joseon enjoyed a prolonged period of peace and prosperity. The increased social mobility and rise in literacy also created conditions necessary for the development of a market for popular fiction written for a mass audience. Unlike the moralistic and esoteric fiction written by *yangban* writers for *yangban* readers, the new works featured exciting and sensational plots that were designed primarily to arouse emotions and to engage interest in the flow of the story line. There are numerous examples of such works—centered around a heroic individual who embarks on a series of action-filled adventures—that were written in the late eighteenth century and throughout the nineteenth century (e.g., *The Story of Jo Ung*, *The Story of So Daeseong*, *The Story of Yu Chungryeol*, and *The Story of Jeon Uchi*, to name just a few) and bear close resemblance to *Hong Gildong jeon* in plot, style, and themes. There is not a single example of that kind of narrative being produced in Joseon prior to the second half of the eighteenth century.

In all probability, the extant work entitled *The Story of Hong Gildong* was written around the middle of the nineteenth century, or not long before that, since the first reference to it in terms of its content, rather than in connection to Yi Sik's attribution of the work to Heo Gyun, does not appear until 1876, in the introduction to an edition of the war fiction *Record of the Black Dragon Year (Imjin rok)*.[8] Its author was likely an anonymous writer of secondary or commoner status, rather than a noble *yangban*, who sought to profit from the market for popular fiction. The work should, therefore, be properly regarded as a mass-market fiction from the late Joseon period, when the dynasty was undergoing one major political and social crisis after another that would lead to its downfall with the Japanese colonization of 1910.

For those who are unfamiliar with traditional East Asian literature, the numerous references in *The Story of Hong Gildong* to Chinese history, philosophy, and literature may give the impression that the writer must have been a highly educated person, perhaps an impoverished *yangban* reduced to writing popular fiction for money. But most of the allusions—like the idyllic state of affairs under the rule of the ancient monarchs Yao and Shun, the literary prowess of the poets Li Bai and Du Mu, and the assassination attempt on the King of Qin by Jing Ke—were so well-known that you did not have to be a particularly learned intellectual to be familiar with them. Comparable examples would be a Western writer's use of Helen of Troy as the symbol of supreme feminine beauty or Alexander the Great as the archetype of a military genius, which would indicate some but not necessarily a high level of education. So the work's literary and historical value should be appreciated in the context of popular rather than elite culture, embodying the desires, anxieties, frustrations, and fantasies of the urban populace of nineteenth-century Korea. With the story's historical context established, it is possible to undertake a proper analysis of its key themes and their engagement with late Joseon culture.

The narrative of *The Story of Hong Gildong* is divided into three parts of near equal lengths, each of them taking place in a completely different environment with its own levels of realism and fantasy. In the opening section, which is set entirely in the compound of the Hong family, there are imaginative descriptions of the dream that High Minister Hong (the father of the hero Hong Gildong) has before conceiving his son, of Hong Gildong's sensational physical and mental abilities, and of the magic he uses to thwart the assassin Teukjae's attempt on his life. Aside from those fantastic elements, the first part provides a highly realistic portrayal of family life in a nobleman's household, complete with a wife, concubines, and children both legitimate and illegitimate. It also paints a convincing portrayal of tensions within the household among its members. For instance, the senior concubine, Chorang, worries that the birth of the extraordinary son by the junior concubine, Chunseom, would cause her to lose the affection of Minister Hong and, consequently, her status in the household hierarchy. This was a legitimate concern that would have plagued such women. But the main drama centers on Hong Gildong's life as a secondary son and the frustrations he feels from his inferior treatment. This has led many scholars to characterize *The Story of Hong Gildong* as protest literature against the Joseon dynasty policy toward illegitimate children.

In the previous dynasty of Goryeo (918–1392), polygamy was legal and widely practiced by elites who could afford to do so. In Joseon, however, Neo-Confucian ideas on family life dictated that a man could have only one legitimate wife. Wealthier men continued to bring extra women into their households as concubines, but these women had no legal standing in society. When a Goryeo man died, all of his wives and their children were eligible to receive a part of his property, but in Joseon only the one wife and her children could claim the inheritance. The number of illegitimate children of the noble *yangban* and their concubines, known as *seoeol* (secondary children), grew rapidly over the course of the dynasty's history as all of their descendants were placed in the secondary social status. *Seoeol* men found themselves in a difficult situation as they grew up in *yangban* households. They became intimate with *yangban* men who were their fathers, half brothers, and friends, and had access to education. But they were not accorded the rights of nobility. As a result, despite their privileged upbringing and high educational level, they often had to depend financially on their relatives or engage in the occupations of commoners to live.

The word denoting the Joseon dynasty nobility, *yangban*, literally means "two orders," signifying the two career paths men of noble families were expected to choose between in order to advance themselves in society. They could take the government's literary examinations (*mungwa*) to enter into civil service or the military examinations (*mugwa*) to join the ranks of military officers. Theoretically, any man of noble, secondary, and commoner status was allowed to take the examinations, but only the *yangban* had the economic wherewithal to provide their sons with the resources—including books, writing implements, and tutors—to devote years of their lives to study for the highly rigorous exams. Even when someone from a non-*yangban* background managed to pass the literary examinations and gained a government post, he found himself stuck in junior positions as he was denied promotion due to prejudice against his background. The eligibility of secondary sons of the *yangban* to take the examinations was a controversial issue throughout the Joseon period.

At the beginning of the dynasty's history, laws were promulgated during the reign of King Taejong (r. 1400–1418) prohibiting secondary sons from taking the civil examinations.[9] In the course of the following centuries, in response to periodic requests by high officials and secondary sons themselves, incremental progress was made in improving the condition of the *seoeol*, though under strict conditions and with limited actual effect. Finally, King Yeongjo (r. 1724–1776), himself the son of a lowborn palace maid, removed all restrictions against secondary children taking the examinations and gave explicit permission for them to address their fathers as Father and older brothers as Brother.[10] Even then, however, they faced considerable obstacles to advancement due to prejudice against their status. It was only in the last decades of the nineteenth century, when the traditional order of Joseon began to fall apart, that secondary sons were able to play significant roles in society and politics.[11]

Among all the works of Joseon fiction, one aspect that makes *The Story of Hong Gildong* unique is its protagonist's status as a secondary son of a nobleman. The hero laments constantly that though he possesses great abilities, he is prohibited from pursuing his ambitions in the traditional *yangban* way because of his birth. Later on, he explains to the King of Joseon that he wanted nothing more than to serve him as a loyal official or a general, and that his frustration at being barred from that course is what caused him to leave home and turn to the life of an outlaw. It is interesting that the work most rivaling *The Story of Hong Gildong* in its popularity and importance to Korean culture is *The Story of Chunhyang*, which is the only fiction that features a protagonist who is a secondary daughter of a nobleman. The persistent popularity of the two works lies in their ability to make the reader identify with the plight of the protagonists through an emotional identification with their frustrations and aspirations. Such feelings would have been felt all the more powerfully by the original audience of secondary and commoner status people who lived in the deeply troubled time of the twilight of the Joseon dynasty, when the established social and political hierarchy fell into severe crisis.

The second part of *The Story of Hong Gildong* narrates the hero's career as the leader of a band of outlaws to whom he gives the name *Hwalbindang* (league of those who help the impoverished). Scholars have regarded this section as the one that is most subversive of the Joseon dynasty order, as it can be read as exposing the corruption and the oppression of the *yangban*-ruled society. There is no doubt that the story features themes that are critical of the status quo, in Hong Gildong's role as a righteous bandit who steals goods and treasures from places that hoard them, and in his acting the part of an official who punishes corrupt magistrates. Such plot elements were no doubt highly attractive to readers who had to deal with corruption and abuse of power by the authorities on a regular basis. This is in line with the archetype of the hero as a champion of the common people, avenging them of the wrongs committed by the rich and the powerful, a universal theme that is characteristic of the "noble robber" figure that can be found in many cultures around the world.[12]

The political dimensions of the narrative may reflect the frustrations of lower-status people who consumed popular fiction, but they can hardly be seen as particularly subversive or revolutionary. Reforming the policy toward secondary sons was an openly discussed topic among *yangban* officials throughout the dynasty's history, and combating corrupt officials for the sake of the common people's well-being was a central concern of traditional Confucian philosophy. No political or social reason is given for the raiding of the Buddhist temple of Haein, other than the presence of a great deal of treasure in the place (the *wanpan* version of the story features an explicitly anti-Buddhist passage related to the raid, but that is a later addition to the text). In fact, in his communications with the King of Joseon, Hong Gildong makes it clear that he had to resort to outlawry because he could not work within the established order as a righteous government official. This shows that his discontentment lies in his inability to participate in the political system of the status quo, not in his ideological antipathy toward its nature. This is a far cry from a revolutionary who wants to overthrow the entire order and replace it with an egalitarian one, as both the fictional hero and his purported creator have so often been depicted in the modern era.

The third part of the story indulges in ever more fantastic adventures. Though the hero's great exploits in foreign lands open up a space outside of traditional Joseon society, the narrative becomes more supportive, rather than subversive, of the status quo. The realms he builds on the islands of Jae and Yul have been described as utopias by many critics, some going so far as to suggest that they reflect the egalitarian state that the purported author Heo Gyun dreamed of building in Joseon. Yet a close reading of the text makes such an interpretation highly problematic.

Ever since Thomas More coined the word "utopia" in the sixteenth century, from Greek root words meaning "no place," it has come to signify not just an optimally functioning society but also one that has achieved such a state through a novel and imaginative arrangement of its community that is different from ones that exist in the world. Due to the influence of Kim Taejun's interpretation of *The Story of Hong Gildong*, people who have never actually read the work might expect some description of an egalitarian system established by Hong Gildong on Yul Island. They might be surprised to find out that there is no such thing in the text, as it offers only a few sparse descriptions of the happy state of its people. After Hong Gildong defeats the King of Yul and ascends the throne, he "ruled with such benevolence that his subjects drummed their full stomachs and sang happy ballads. 'A time of peace and prosperity has come, like in the days of Yo and Sun.'" The last two names are references to Yao and Shun, two semimythical rulers of ancient China who were regarded as ideal monarchs. Later on, after the episode involving the death of Hong Gildong's mother, it is related that "Through the benevolent rule of the king, the country was at peace and saw rich harvests, the people feeling secure with their households well stocked. No inauspicious incident disturbed the country." These passages are the entirety of the descriptions of the state of Yul Island under Hong Gildong's rule. In actuality, they are nothing more than depictions of people's contentment under the reign of a good and able monarch, not of a novel system of governance to which the word "utopia" could be applied. In other words, there is no evidence to support the idea that the story tells of a state with a political and social system radically different from Joseon's, one devoid of hierarchy or caste.

What Hong Gildong establishes on Yul Island is, in fact, a kingdom with himself as an absolute monarch, and references to the titles he grants his officials indicate that he essentially replicates the Joseon political system in his realm. He also adopts the one-legitimate-wife-per-man policy as he makes one of the women he rescued from the *uldong* monsters his wife but takes the other two as his concubines. The secondary sons by the concubines are given the ranks of *gun* (a royal title for a prince) and *bek* (the highest rank of nobility) and sent out to live on Jae Island, which evidently becomes a subordinate territory to Yul Island. It is as if Hong Gildong the king has completely forgotten his earlier frustrations as a secondary son. This points to the traditional nature of the narrative, which depicts the aspirations and the ultimate success of the hero in Confucian and monarchist terms. It would be highly anachronistic then to depict Hong's kingdom as revolutionary or utopian, rather than seeing it in the proper historical context of a Joseon dynasty fantasy of an idyllic land ruled over by an ideal king who is modeled after monarchs of ancient, mythical times.

Whatever kind of political interpretation can be made of the work, its central purpose is not one of ideological advocacy. The moving portrayal of the hero's frustration as a secondary son, his role as the leader of outlaws, and his challenges against authority figures, from local officials to the king, can all be read as critiques of the status quo. But one must also consider the fact that Hong Gildong's ambitions are always couched in traditional terms of desiring to work as a government official. As an intrepid and invincible leader of loyal bandits, he never seriously tries to change the society he lives in, and he ultimately submits to his monarch once he is granted an official position. *The Story of Hong Gildong* is first and foremost a narrative of entertainment about an extraordinary hero who achieves great things despite the initial disadvantage of his birth.

Ultimately, *The Story of Hong Gildong* should be appreciated not only as one of the best prose narratives produced during the Joseon dynasty, but also as the finest example of popular fiction that appeared in the course of the late eighteenth century and throughout the nineteenth. As a product of the last period of the dynasty, the work differs significantly from the moralistic fiction by *yangban* writers in that it is a plot-driven narrative featuring fast-paced episodes that alternate between scenes of high emotion and exciting action. All available evidence points to the fact that it was originally composed in the phonetic *hangeul* script to accommodate the increasing number of literate common people.

The work's persistent popularity in the modern era can be explained by its elevation of a neglected secondary son as a great hero. In the history of modern Korea, the people of the peninsula have experienced a series of humiliations from colonization, forced division, and domestic oppression. As a result, a central agenda in the political rhetoric of both North and South Korea has been the recovery of national dignity and respect, oftentimes through massive displays of newly acquired power in the realms of the military, economy, and culture. Starting from the attempt by imperial Japan to convince Koreans that they were inferior relatives who had to be civilized through colonial tutelage, the liberated but soon divided nations felt like the bastard children of foreign powers that set their destinies in motion without consulting them on their own desires for the future. As a result, the theme of being disrespected, unappreciated, and underrated by callous and unwise authority figures blind to the emotional needs and the substantial talents of the protagonist, so well portrayed in the first part of *The Story of Hong Gildong*, has a profound resonance in the Korean psyche. In other words, the Joseon dynasty story of a secondary son seeking to overcome the disadvantages of his background and the oppression of his society in order to prove his true worth as a man, a leader, and a ruler has become the story of modern Korea itself.

MINSOO KANG

A Note on the Translation

The immediate problem that a prospective translator of *The Story of Hong Gildong* has to face is the existence of no less than thirty-four extant manuscripts, most of them featuring textual differences of varying degrees. To give some examples, the longest version of the work (the *pilsa* 89) is five times the length of the shortest (the *gyeongpan* 17). Some feature extended passages not found in others, like an anti-Buddhist passage and fuller descriptions of the final battle in the *wanpan* versions. And there are numerous minor variations in details, for instance the *gyeongpan* texts identify the highest government post gained by Hong Gildong's father as the minister of personnel (*ijo panseo*), whereas the *wanpan* texts have him as the state councilor of the left (*jwa uijeong*) and the *pilsa* texts have him as the state councilor of the right (*u uijeong*). The question of which text is the ur-text or the closest to it is a difficult one to answer since only fifteen of them feature definitive dates of publication, ranging from 1893 to 1936. Lee Yoon Suk, however, has made an exhaustive study of extant variants, coming to the conclusion that the *pilsa* 89 version is the oldest.[1]

Korean printers of the nineteenth and early twentieth centuries did not solicit original works to publish, but took handwritten works that were enjoying popularity and put out printed versions. Further, once a work achieved success in the marketplace, both copiers and printers produced abbreviated versions of the text in order to save money on production, especially on the cost of paper. Given such publishing practices of the time, the longer handwritten versions of a given work can generally be regarded as earlier versions. The *pilsa* (handwritten) text Kim Donguk 89 is the longest variant of *The Story of Hong Gildong* that has survived. This is the version that many contemporary scholars believe to be either a copy of the ur-text or the one closest in content to it.

Of the thirty-four extant texts, twenty-five were handwritten and nine printed. The printed texts were produced in the three centers of the printing industry in nineteenth- and early-twentieth-century Korea—Gyeongseong (today's Seoul), Wanju (today's Jeonju in North Jeolla Province), and Anseong (in Gyeonggi Province, south of Seoul). So the printed works are referred to as *gyeongpan*, *wanpan*, and *anseongpan*, the syllable *pan* denoting a wooden or metal plate that was used for printing. The numerals attached to each text indicate the number of standard-size sheets used, providing a general idea of the length of the narrative. So, the *gyeongpan* 24 is a printed text of twenty-four sheets that was published in Gyeongseong, while *wanpan* 36 is in thirty-six pages and was published in Wanju. The handwritten manuscripts are referred to by the name of the person who owns a particular text or the institution where it is housed, followed by the sheet count. So, the Park Sunho 86 is a handwritten text of eighty-six sheets held in the private collection of Park Sunho, while the Tōyō bunko 31/31/33 is a work in three volumes of thirty-one, thirty-one, and thirty-three sheets, respectively, that is at the Tōyō bunko (Asian Studies) library in Tokyo, Japan.

The most commonly used English translation is Marshall Pihl's, which was first published in *Korean Journal* in 1968 and reprinted in Peter H. Lee's 1981 *Anthology of Korean Literature*.[2] It is a rendering of the *gyeongpan* 24, one of the shortest variants, which was thought at the time to be the authoritative version but is now considered by scholars to be abbreviated from *gyeongpan* 30. What follows here is a translation of the longest and probably the oldest of the surviving manuscripts, the *pilsa* 89.

I have also chosen to use the new revised system of romanization that was introduced in 2000 by the Republic of Korea's Ministry of Culture, now the standard in South Korea, rather than the older McCune-Reischauer system. I have found the new system to do a better job of expressing the sounds of *hangeul* characters. It also does away with the diacritical marks of McCune-Reischauer, which gave transliterations a technical look that is intimidating to readers unfamiliar with Korean literature and scholarship.

The Story of
Hong Gildong

In the time of the ascension of King Seonjong¹ the Great to the throne of Joseon, there lived a state minister in the city of Jangan² whose family name was Hong and whose personal name was *mo*.³ His progenitors had attained lofty positions in the royal court and had maintained great wealth for generations, so they were renowned throughout the country for their illustrious nobility. He passed the civil service examinations at a young age and reached the position of high minister⁴ in the government, where his reputation for integrity and moral courage earned him the special favor of the king. He had a son named Inhyeon who also passed the examinations early and gained the rank of assistant section chief⁵ at the Ministry of Personnel.⁶ He too received the attention of his sovereign.

On a warm spring day, the minister was suddenly overcome by fatigue and fell into a dream. He found himself in a place where verdant mountains lay in multiple folds, fresh waters flowed gently, and willow branches were arrayed like so many canopies of green. In the midst of the fairest panorama, golden songbirds calling for their mates evoked the pleasures of spring. Awed by the grandeur of the scenery, the minister strolled through the land until the path he walked on ended at a rocky cliff that soared up to pierce the sky. A waterfall that fell from a height looked like a white dragon at play, and the mountain's stone wall of ten thousand *jang*⁷ was covered in many-colored clouds. Filled with joy at finding himself in such a marvelous world, the minister sat on a rock to fully appreciate the beauty all around him. Suddenly, deaf-ening explosions of thunder shook heaven and earth, the waters rose up in tumultuous eruptions, and a fierce tempest blew through the land. A blue dragon appeared, shaking its beard, glaring with its frightful eyes, and opening wide its red mouth as it rushed at the minister to hunt him down. Taking great fright, he tried to flee from the creature but it quickly enveloped him. He woke up then and realized that it had all been a dream.

The minister felt a great happiness in his heart,[8] and he imme-diately entered the inner chamber[9] of his house, where his wife stood up to greet him. With a delighted expression on his face, he led her to the resting place of the room. There he took her exquisite hands and made apparent his intention to become one with her in a decorous manner.

But his wife's delicate features turned serious as she spoke to him. "Your Lordship is a person of high position in the world and no longer a young man of excessive vitality. So why are you acting like a licentious youth in broad daylight and in view of the maids who spy upon this chamber? For the sake of your dignity, I will not comply with your desire." She withdrew her hands, opened the chamber's door, and walked out.

The minister felt embarrassed by the situation and considered explaining his behavior by telling her of the dream. But he resisted the urge as he felt that it was wrong to divulge a secret vision heaven had granted him. Unable to allay his frustration, he went to the outer chamber with an upset expression as he lamented his wife's lack of understanding. It was then that a maid named Chunseom entered the room to serve him tea. After the minister took his drink, he saw that all was quiet in the household, so he took Chunseom's hand and led her into a side chamber where he lay with her. She was a girl of nineteen years at the time.

Although Chunseom was only a servant girl, she had a gentle nature and her demeanor and actions were always as proper as those of a respectable maiden. She may have been lowborn, but there was nothing lowly about her character. When the minister approached her so suddenly with an authoritative air and made apparent his ardent desire for her, she dared not resist his advance and allowed him the use of her body. From that day on she never ventured outside the house and showed no interest in other men. The minister was so impressed by her loyalty that he made her a concubine.[10]

Within a month, Chunseom began to show signs of being with child, which earned her the animosity of a senior concubine whose name was Chorang. The latter was a person of wicked character who became filled with jealousy when she learned of the pregnancy. She dared not reveal her feelings in words or looks, but she resented the minister for his actions and regarded Chunseom with hatred.

And so time passed, through ten lunar months,[11] until a day came when a tempest blew, fierce rain poured down, and a fragrant air filled the house. Chunseom gave birth to a precious boy whose face was the color of snow and whose presence was as grand as the autumn moon. He was born with the appearance of a great hero. The minister was delighted and granted him the name of Gildong.

As the boy grew up, he exhibited magnificence in both the strength of his body and the brilliance of his intellect. He needed to hear only one thing to understand ten,[12] and learning ten things allowed him to master a hundred. He never forgot a single thing he heard or saw just once.

But the minister had cause to lament his fate. "The will of Heaven can be so callous. How could it allow such a heroic personage to be born of a servant girl and not of a proper wife?" He often grieved over this.

When Gildong was five years old, the minister took his hand and complained to his wife. "You were disobedient to me once, so you must bear the responsibility for this situation."

His wife smiled and asked him to explain. The minister frowned and let out a deep sigh before answering her. "If you had heeded me in the past, this child would have been born of your body." It was only then that he told her of the dream.

His wife bewailed the lost fortune, but there was nothing they could do to change what fate had ordained.

Years went by and Gildong reached his eighth year, exhibiting ever greater talent and refinement of character. He was adored by his family, but the concubine Chorang continued to regard him with envy that pained her in the pit of her stomach night and day. The minister loved Gildong greatly, but because he was born of a mere servant girl he was punished with a switch to the legs if he dared to call him Father.[13] The minister also frowned at Gildong if he addressed his older brother as Brother, and prohibited him from doing so. This became a source of great sorrow for Gildong, who constantly lamented that he could not properly acknowledge his own father and brother, and had to endure contemptuous treatment in the household, all because he was lowborn.

One night, in the middle of the ninth lunar month, the blue sky was illuminated by a full moon and a chilly wind of autumn blew—an atmosphere that enhances the joy of a happy person but exacerbates the melancholy of a troubled one. Gildong was studying in his room when he pushed aside his reading table and sighed out loud. "Born as a true man into this world, if I cannot follow the virtuous path of Gongja and Maengja,[14] then I would go forth to become a general and rise up as a high minister. I would wear a moon-sized insignia of a commander on my waist and sit upon a high seat from which I would order a thousand men and ten thousand horses to conquer the east and subdue the west. In such a way I would do great service to the country and achieve glory. I would then be elevated to become the loftiest of men below the king. And as a high minister I would work for the country with utmost loyalty so that my name would become renowned for generations and my portrait memorialized in Girin House.[15] That would be the fulfillment of a man's happiness. The ancients have said, 'Kings, lords, generals, and ministers are not made from a special blood.'[16] But for whose benefit was such a thing said? I have been born into a situation in which I am barred from following my ambitions, and I cannot even address my father as Father and my older brother as Brother." Overcome with profound sorrow, he could not stop his tears from flowing.

He got up and wandered about the stone stairs of the court-yard, where he performed a sword dance beneath the moon's shadows. His father, the minister, loved the fragrance of the night air in autumn, so he opened his window to gaze at the moon's hue. When Gildong heard him, he threw away his sword and went before him.

The minister questioned him. "What are you doing prowl-ing about in the middle of the night?"

Gildong answered him. "I came out to enjoy the moonlight."

The minister sighed and questioned him further. "What pos-sessed you to be out there?"

Gildong replied in a humble manner. "Of all things created by Heaven, a human being is the most precious. So it is the most fortunate thing to be born a human in this world. And being born a human, it is the most fortunate thing to be born a man. And being born a man, it is the most fortunate thing to be born in the capital city. In addition to those three fortunes, I have inherited Your Lordship's abundant spirit and strength, and I have grown up to become a sturdy man. You have shown me nothing but deep and constant love, so I should have nothing to resent in the world. Yet all my life I have had to bear this sorrow inside me which prevents me from looking up at Heaven with pride." Two trails of tears wet Gildong's red cheeks as he spoke.

The minister felt great pity for him. As he considered the boy who was less than ten years old but who could already foresee the fortunes of his entire life, he feared that expressing sympathy for his plight would aggravate his discontent. So he admonished him loudly. "You are hardly the only lowborn child in a high minister's family. How can such a young boy harbor such a great resentment? If you ever speak of this mat-ter again you will be severely punished."

Gildong could only shed more tears at the minister's words as he prostrated himself over a banister in grief. After a while, the minister ordered him away, so he went to his sleeping chamber, where he could hardly console himself.

Several months later, Gildong went to the west pavilion to ask the minister a question. "If I may be so bold as to inquire, I know that I am but a lowborn person, but why is it that I excel in writing yet I am not allowed to take the civil examinations in the hope of one day becoming a government minister? And why is it that I am proficient in archery yet I am not allowed to take the military examinations in the hope of one day becoming a general?"

The minister reprimanded him loudly. "I told you before not to utter such resentful words, so how dare you do so now?"

He dismissed him with this admonishment, so Gildong went to his mother to speak to her. "During my time on earth I would go forth to make a name for myself, to bring glory to my parents' names and to conduct proper rites for my ancestors. Yet because of the misfortune of my birth I am treated with low regard by relatives and neighbors alike. Only Heaven knows the depth of the sorrow I harbor in my heart. How can a true man resign himself to being considered an inferior by others all his life? All I want is the opportunity to advance myself in the proper way, to enter government service and eventually become a high general in the hope of one day receiving the royal insignia[17] of the minister of war. But since I am prohibited from pursuing such an ambition, I fear that I may end up leaving home and perhaps committing some unrighteous act for which I will remain notorious even after my death. Mother, should I ever find myself in a situation that forces me to leave your side, please hide your love for me deep within you and wait patiently for my return."

Chunseom replied, "You are hardly the only lowborn child in a high minister's family. Why do you bear such resentment and think nothing of hurting your mother's feelings? You must try to accept your lot in life for my sake."

Gildong responded, "Even the household servants regard me with contempt and speak of me as so-and-so's lowborn child. Every time that happens, the pain of my condition affects me to the marrow of my bones. Long ago, Jang Chung's son Gilsan[18] was born of a servant girl as well, but he took leave of his mother and went up Ungbong Mountain to practice the Way[19] and became renowned for generations. I plan to follow his path one day. So I beg you to forget me for a time, until we are reunited in the future when I will try to repay you for all the love you have shown me in what paltry way I can. Also, I think Mother Goksan[20] is taking advantage of His Lordship's favor to plot against you in some way, so I fear that something unseemly might soon occur."

Chunseom replied, "I understand the reason behind your words, but Mother Goksan is a good and kindly person. I cannot believe she would be capable of such a thing."

"The inner thought of another is not something that can be easily discerned. So I ask you to be vigilant in the coming days and take measures to protect yourself."

As Chunseom listened to Gildong's many troubles she felt great sadness, but there was nothing mother and son could do but console each other.

The minister's senior concubine, Chorang, was originally a courtesan[21] from the town of Goksan. Because she was beloved by the minister above all, she enjoyed the greatest favors and wielded the greatest influence in the family. She was a fiendish person to start with and became ever more arrogant. Every time some trouble occurred in the household, she would always cause mischief by going to the minister and slandering those she did not like. She gained even more power that way. Whenever someone was brought down she rejoiced in her heart, but whenever someone was raised up she became jealous and considered that person an enemy. After the minister received the dragon dream and Gildong was born, Chorang saw that he loved the boy for his extraordinary qualities. Just when she began to hate Chunseom from the worry that the minister would now favor the younger concubine, he began to say to her with a smile—"You too should bring me happiness by giving me such a magnificent child."

But as much as Chorang wished to have a son of her own, she ended up with no children at all. And so she came to despise Gildong to the extent of plotting his murder every single day.

As Gildong continued to grow, his talents surpassed those of adults and his bearing came to resemble that of Yi Taebaek and Du Mok.[22] People could not help but compliment Gildong on his qualities, so Chorang's jealousy grew. She gathered a great deal of money and consulted with diabolical and treacherous women like shamans and physiognomists[23] on how to harm Gildong.

Chorang addressed them. "If you will bring me peace by getting rid of Gildong, I will reward you handsomely."

One shaman, out of sheer greed for the wealth Chorang offered, came up with a wicked stratagem. She explained her plan to Chorang. "His Lordship is a superior man of great loyalty to the country and personal piety, but he is so busy with the affairs of state that he is hardly aware of what is going on in his own household. You should take advantage of this. You should consult a first-class physiognomist I know who lives outside Sungrye Gate.[24] She is reputed to possess the power to fathom all the fortunes and misfortunes of a person's past and future by looking at the face just once. You should hire her, inform her of your wish, and recommend her to His Lordship so that she will go before him to practice her craft. She could then pretend to read his fortune and tell him something that would impress him enough to get rid of that boy. If executed step-by-step at the right time, this plan is bound to succeed."

Chorang was pleased by the shaman's words. "That is the cleverest and most marvelous plan I have ever heard. Go and speak to that physiognomist," she said and immediately gave her fifty *nyang*[25] in silver coins. The shaman took the money, went to the house of the physiognomist, and told her of Chorang's situation. She then offered her the silver coins, which the physiognomist accepted as she too was a greedy woman.

She looked at the money and thought to herself, "I am given this much to start off with. I will surely receive even greater favors when the plan is accomplished." So she readily followed the shaman to the house of Minister Hong without once considering the consequences of getting involved in such a matter. Chorang welcomed her by serving her spirits and delicacies before revealing her wish. After the physiognomist learned of the plot that was being hatched, she returned home.

The next day, the minister was sitting with his wife when he began to praise Gildong. "That boy possesses the grand features of an outstanding person. It is obvious that he was meant to lead a life of great destiny. It is a pity that he is lowborn."

His wife was about to reply honestly to the comment, when a woman suddenly appeared and prostrated herself before them.

"Who are you, and what business do you have here?" the minister asked her, noting the strangeness of her appearance.

The woman answered, "Once I lived outside Sungrye Gate, but due to an unfortunate fate I lost both my parents at the age of eight and became an orphan with no one to rely on. I wandered about in all directions without a home to go to, until I met a holy man who taught me the magical art of physiognomy, by which I can read the fortunes and misfortunes of any person. I happened upon the gates of Your Lordship's house, so I have come before you to offer my services."

The minister's wife wanted to see the woman practice her craft, so she magnanimously invited her to sit with them.

The minister smiled as he addressed the physiognomist. "If you are good at reading people's faces, then I will have the people of my household come before you one by one so you can tell their fortunes."

The physiognomist was pleased that her plan was coming to fruition as she proceeded to examine the facial features of all the members of the household, high and low, and made critical remarks on their characters and told their fortunes. Her assessments of their personalities were so accurate that she earned profuse praise from the minister and his wife, who complimented her wondrous skills.

They summoned Gildong and introduced him to her. "This child came to us rather late, and our love for him knows no limit. Look at him closely and tell us of his future."

The physiognomist examined him for some time before she bowed down and spoke. "When I look upon this noble youth, I see that he possesses the extraordinary features of a grand personage of unprecedented refinement as well as the luminous qualities of a veritable hero. Yet I also detect a misfortune in his lack of proper lineage, which makes it difficult for me to read his future properly. Was he born of your wife?"

The minister nodded in understanding and replied, "He was born of a servant girl, one I love for her simple and honest nature."

The physiognomist then looked upon Gildong's face again and pretended to be shocked by what she discerned.

The minister found her reaction strange so he questioned her. "What is it? Tell me everything you see."

The physiognomist deliberately hesitated before answering him. "I have visited countless households of both lofty and common people in the city of Jangan and examined so many precious and noble youths, but I have never seen a person of such phenomenal visage as his. But I fear that I would be punished if I were to tell Your Lordship all that I see."

The minister's wife spoke. "With your uncanny powers, how could you go wrong in your reading? Lay aside your worry and tell us the whole truth."

The physiognomist feigned concern that there were too many people around to listen and refused to answer. So the minister got up and took her inside a side chamber, where he bade her speak. "What is it? Tell me everything."

The physiognomist answered, "When I gazed briefly upon the noble youth's face, I saw not only the magnificent features of a grand personage without equal but also the spirit of rivers and mountains deep in his brow. So I dared not tell you of the truly remarkable nature that I discerned in your son. Joseon is a small country, so what use is it for him to possess the qualities of a king? If he should grow up to harbor a great ambition that leads him to engage in outright rebellion, that could cause the destruction of your entire family.[26] Your Lordship should take measures to prevent such a thing from happening."

The minister was so shocked by those words that he could not speak for a while.

When he finally regained his voice he addressed the physiognomist. "If that is true, then it is a great misfortune indeed. But whatever fate may have in store for him, he could never enter the ranks of the nobility because he was born of a servant girl. Perhaps I could forestall calamity by forbidding him from ever leaving this house. And so he would grow old here without ever having the opportunity to cause mischief in the world."

She replied, "The ancients have said, 'Kings, lords, generals, and ministers are not made from a special blood,'[27] so his destiny is not something that can be altered through mere human effort."

The minister let out a sigh and gave the physiognomist fifty *nyang* as he spoke to her. "I give you this for what you have told me, but do not divulge what you know to anyone. I will punish you if a word of what you have said becomes known."

The physiognomist expressed her gratitude and left.

From that day on, the minister treated Gildong with strictness and kept a close eye on everything he did. He was ordered to concentrate on his studies and was prohibited from venturing outside. He was also confined to a small cottage in the rear garden, which suppressed his natural spirit. This caused him to weep bitterly in frustration. He dedicated himself to studying military treatises, including the *Six Teachings* and the *Three Summaries*,[28] and mastering astrology, geomancy,[29] and the magical arts of invisibility and metamorphosis. He assimilated all this knowledge so thoroughly in his mind that there was no task that was impossible for him.

As the minister monitored the progress of his son's studies, he became concerned. "He is indeed a special person since his talents are not those of an ordinary man. If he should conceive a great ambition for himself, then surely misfortune would follow. Our family has served the country with utmost fidelity for generations, adhering to the principles of loyalty and filial piety. But all that could come to nothing overnight if he should commit an action that causes our downfall. What a terrible situation this is. To prevent such a thing from happening, I should have him killed."

The minister considered summoning his entire family to explain the situation and to order them to quietly get rid of Gildong. But he was moved by his moral sensibility and could not bring himself to do so.

Meanwhile, the alliance of Chorang, the shaman, and the physiognomist met daily to discuss plans to further subvert the relationship between the minister and his son, to continue to slander the latter and bring about his death.

The shaman addressed Chorang. "There is an assassin by the name of Teukjae who is said to possess great skills. You should summon him and consult him on this matter."

Chorang was pleased to hear this and asked her to bring this Teukjae to her. She gave the assassin many silver coins and told him of what the physiognomist discerned in Gildong's face. She also informed him that the minister considered getting rid of his son but could not do so because of moral qualms. "But I will order you to do the deed at some point in time, and you will go ahead and make it happen," she said and sent him on his way.

She then went to the minister to malign Gildong. "I have heard that the physiognomist discerned the spirit of a king in Gildong's face. I am afraid that our entire family will be destroyed because of that."

The minister was astonished by her words and addressed her. "That is a highly serious matter. How dare you speak of it openly and invite misfortune."

Chorang replied in a concerned manner. "As the saying goes, 'What is said in daytime is overheard by the bird, and what is said in nighttime is overheard by the rat.'[30] I tremble at the thought of word reaching the government of what the physiognomist saw in Gildong. If that should happen, none of us would survive. It seems to me that the right thing to do is to have Gildong killed quickly to prevent future calamity."

The minister replied, "What you say may be right, but this is a matter for me to decide. Do not speak of it to anyone."

Chorang dared not go on, so she left.

From that day on, the minister treated Gildong with even greater strictness, continuing to confine him to the small cottage in the rear garden and prohibiting him from venturing outside. Gildong felt such sorrow and frustration deep in his bones that he could hardly sleep at night. He spent much of his time at his reading table and mastered the *Juyeok*[31] until he gained the power to summon supernatural spirits and control the wind and the rain.

Even though the minister still loved Gildong for his noble qualities and his abundant talents, he periodically thought of the physiognomist's words and became concerned. He thought to himself, "This unfortunate son of mine could one day cause a disaster to fall upon me, bringing dishonor to our ancestors and destruction to three generations of the family. It would be wise to dispose of him to avoid this course, but I just cannot set aside my love for him as his father. So what must I do?" Plagued by such worries, he could neither taste his food nor sleep soundly at night, which made him look increasingly haggard from day to day. Finally, he fell ill. The minister's wife and their son, the assistant section chief,[32] became deeply troubled and spoke to each other discreetly about the situation. They agreed that given the minister's condition, the best thing would be to allay his anxiety by getting rid of Gildong. But they could not bring themselves to do it, so they grieved over the situation.

At this time, Chorang, who continued to malign Gildong, conceived an evil plan and went before the minister's wife and the assistant section chief. "Every day His Lordship's condition grows worse because of Gildong. Keeping the boy alive will

surely result in calamity, but His Lordship cannot bring himself
to dispose of him because of his affection for him. So he is tor-
mented by his indecision. In my opinion, you should have Gildong killed and then eventually reveal the deed to His Lordship
under the right circumstances, so that he would have no choice
but to accept the broken steamer.[33] That would cause him grief,
but it would also free him from his greatest anxiety. He would
surely recover his health as a result. You should consider this
matter carefully."

The minister's wife replied, "Even if what you say is right,
how could we do it?"

Chorang, secretly pleased, answered her. "I have heard that
there is an assassin by the name of Teukjae who lives in this neigh-
borhood. He is reputed to be a man of great courage. You should
give him a good deal of money to steal into Gildong's sleeping
chamber at night and do the deed. That would be a good plan."

Both the assistant section chief and his mother broke into
tears before the former spoke. "I dare not do such an inhuman
thing. But then again, this is a matter of the welfare of the entire
country as well as my parents. So how could I not do it?" He
finally told Chorang to go ahead with the plan, which brought
her joy.

She went to her chamber and sent a servant out to summon
Teukjae. When he came, she presented him with an array of
spirits and delicacies to enjoy. She explained everything that
had happened and gave him instructions on what to do. "This
order comes from His Lordship and his wife. Tonight, on the
third or fourth watch,[34] go to the rear garden and put an end
to Gildong's life. If you succeed, I will reward you with a great
deal of money." She then gave him silver coins worth a hundred *nyang*, which pleased Teukjae.

He addressed her. "This is not a difficult task for me. Set
aside your worry." He then left to wait for the night.

After Chorang sent Teukjae away, she immediately returned
to the inner chamber of the house and explained what she had
set in motion.

The minister's wife heard her out before she let out a sigh. "I do this not because I have any animosity toward Gildong but because it was a necessary thing to do for the sake of the family. But how could I be honored by my descendants when I have committed such a heinous act?" And she wept without restraint.

The assistant section chief sighed and consoled her. "Mother, please do not be so sad. We did what was necessary, so there is no use regretting it. I will take good care of Gildong's body and dress it in the finest silk, and I will also treat his mother with generosity. After Father finds out what happened, he will eventually come to accept it and he will surely recover his health. So please do not grieve so much."

But the minister's wife could not sleep at all that night because her mind was full of regret and anxiety.

Meanwhile, Gildong sat forlornly in his cottage, studying the *Juyeok* by candlelight, until the night reached the third watch. Realizing how late it was, he was about to set aside his reading table and go to sleep when he saw a raven come flying from the south, caw three times in front of his room, and then fly north.

Gildong considered its cries and thought, "That bird does not like to venture out at night, so it is very strange that it should fly from the south at this time and head north." He quickly cast his fortune by consulting ancient ideograms and discovered that the raven's cries spoke of the approach of a killer. "Who could be so reckless as to come to harm me?" he wondered and cast another divinatory spell, which produced a piece of paper with a magical symbol that he pulled out of his sleeve. It denoted an aspect of great evil, so Gildong pondered it before saying to himself, "Whatever happens, I must prepare a defense against an intruder." He then unleashed his sorcery[35] and attached the fire trigram of the southward direction to the northward direction, the water trigram of the northward direction to the southward direction, the thunder trigram of the eastward direction to the westward direction, the lake trigram of the westward direction to the eastward direction, the heaven trigram of the northwestward direction to the southeastward direction, the wind trigram of the southeastward direction to the northwestward direction, the mountain trigram of the northeastward direction to the south-westward direction, and the earth trigram of the southwestward direction to the northeastward direction. And so he used his magic to change all the directional orientation inside the cottage. He then summoned a supernatural spirit and ordered it to await his command in the middle of the room. Such were the marvelous powers Gildong possessed.

Meanwhile, Teukjae waited until it was third watch before he took up his dagger and went forth. He used his martial prowess to leap into the air and jump over the wall of the Hong family compound into the rear garden, where he spied upon Gildong's cottage. The view inside the silk-covered window was obscure and there was no sound of anyone about, so he waited for Gil-dong to fall asleep. Suddenly, a raven came flying from the south, cawed in front of the house, and flew north.

Teukjae talked to himself in astonishment. "It is true that Gil-dong is no ordinary person. That bird came to tell him some-thing. If Gildong has received a warning of what is about to happen, this could go terribly wrong."

And so he waited for Gildong to retire, but the light inside never went out. He finally opened the door and peeked within to see a noble youth sitting upright by the light of a candle. Teukjae decided to kill him right then and there, so he gripped his dagger and slipped into the chamber. Gildong remained still as he cast spells using the eight trigrams, raising a dreadful wind that confused Teukjae's mind.

The assassin spoke to himself in bewilderment. "I have never felt fear even in the direst situation, so why am I filled with ter-ror now?" He tried to recover his composure by thinking, "Ever since I became a master of my skills, I have never made a single mistake. How could I retreat now, fearing a small boy?"

And so he raised his dagger and cautiously went forth to com-mit his act, but then he found that Gildong had disappeared without a trace. Suddenly, a fearsome wind blew and thunder-claps shook heaven and earth. The room then transformed itself into an immense field filled with countless rocks, layers of green mountains that soared into the air with intimidating grandeur, and rivers that flowed gently through valleys. An abundance of blue pine trees made the scenery all the more fair.

Teukjae tried to orient himself in the strange environment as he thought, "A moment ago I went into Gildong's room to kill him, so how did I come to this mountainous place?"

He looked around and found a path stretched out before him, but because he had no idea where to go and had lost all sense of direction, he ended up falling over himself. After he wandered about for a while, he sat down by a stream and lamented. "I am in this situation because I underestimated Gildong. I have no one to blame but myself. All this is undoubtedly the work of his uncanny powers."

He then put away his dagger and followed the stream until the path ended at a rocky cliff that fell precipitously into a void. As he could go no farther, he rested on the rocky ground. Suddenly, he heard a melancholy tune from a jade flute reverberating in the wind. He looked around for the source of the eerie sound until he saw a young boy playing the instrument.

The youth stopped to reprimand him in a loud voice. "You ignorant, wicked, lowly wretch, listen to me carefully. Holy men have said, 'A human life is so precious that even if you destroy a wooden object in the shape of a person that counts as an evil act that deserves punishment.' So what kind of a person are you that you would proceed so recklessly to murder an innocent person, all out of greed for wealth? I may only be a boy of three *cheok*,[36] but I will never allow someone like you to end me. In ancient times, for all the courage the Supreme King of Cho[37] possessed, he failed to cross O River and ended up a ghost beneath a lonely mast. And for all the swiftness of Hyeong Gyeong's sword,[38] he ended up floating on the cold water of Yeok River. So how did such an insignificant creature like you imagine that you could leave my room alive? You value only money and think nothing of taking a person's life, so you bring doom upon yourself. Pitiful man, do you not fear the judgment of Heaven?"

Teukjae looked at the boy with trepidation and saw that it was none other than Gildong. He thought to himself, "Because of him I may end up losing all the strength I have accumulated throughout my lifetime. But even if I should meet my death tonight, how could a true man surrender himself to a child?"

He calmed himself before replying forcefully, "For ten years now I have honed my fighting skills, and there is no rival who is my equal. I have come to kill you under the order of your father and older brother. You have no cause to reprimand or ridicule me. Do not resent me for your impending death, but rather obey your father and older brother and submit yourself to their will."

As soon as he finished speaking, he ran toward Gildong in a sword dance with his dagger raised to strike. Gildong, in his fury, wanted to kill him right then and there, but he did not have a weapon in hand, so he quickly flew into the air in the embrace of a wind spirit. He then cast a spell that sent dirt and pebbles flying at Teukjae, who could not keep his eyes open or nostrils exposed. When Teukjae finally managed to look around, he found that Gildong had disappeared once again. Filled with awe at Gildong's power, he wanted to flee but did not know which way to go.

A moment later, Gildong suddenly addressed him in a booming voice. "There was never a cause for us to become enemies, so why are you trying to kill me? I gave you a chance to listen to reason and let me be, but out of greed you have chosen to bring death upon yourself."

It was only then that Teukjae understood the full extent of Gildong's powers, so he approached him in a posture of surrender while pleading, "I am not the only one guilty of this transgression against you since this whole plot was conceived by His Lordship's young lady Chorang. She planned your death with a shaman and a physiognomist, slandered you to your father, and then told me, 'If you kill the noble son and so prevent future calamity from falling upon our family you will be rewarded with a thousand gold coins.' But Heaven has decreed that all this should come to light. I beg you to forgive me, noble sir."

Unable to suppress his rage, Gildong took Teukjae's blade away from him and scolded him bitterly. "You commit evil acts that involve murdering human beings. How did you think you could avoid the judgment of Heaven? If I spare you, many others will die. By killing you I will be saving lives."

He then raised the weapon and cut Teukjae down, causing a line of rainbow to flash as the assassin's decapitated head fell in the middle of the room. Still filled with a fury that he could not allay, Gildong summoned the wind spirit again and sent it forth to grab the shaman and the physiognomist in a tempest and bring them to the chamber where Teukjae had met his death. The shaman and the physiognomist were disoriented in their sleepy state and wondered if they had fallen into the underworld.

Gildong scolded them. "Do you know who I am? I am Hong Gildong himself. I have done nothing to cause you to hate me. Why did you wretches utter such slanderous words to His Lordship, to cause disharmony in the natural bond between father and son? How could such a thing be forgiven?"

At first, the shaman and the physiognomist thought they were in a dream where their souls were lifted up and borne gently forth by a great wind to a far and unknown place. They were lost in bewilderment all the while. But when they heard Gildong's words, they finally realized that they were not in the afterlife but still in the living world, where they were brought before a human being.

They pleaded with him. "All this is the work of His Lordship's concubine Chorang. Now that you know this, we humbly beg you, noble sir, to forgive us and let us live out the rest of our sorry lives."

Gildong replied in anger. "Chorang is His Lordship's beloved, and she is a mother to me as well. You lowly creatures dared to use wicked talk to instigate trouble. You toyed with the state of a high minister's household. How could you evade the judgment of Heaven? Heaven commands me to rid the world of the likes of you to prevent further mischief you may cause. Do not resent me for it." And he cut them down with his blade.

It was a terrible scene indeed! Losing one's life as a result of committing an immoral act of greed, one incurs the shame of a thousand years. How pitiful that is.

After he killed the shaman and the physiognomist, Gildong still could not allay his wrath, so he started for the inner chamber of the house to kill Chorang. But then he thought to himself, "I may have been treated badly by another, but I will not reciprocate the deed. She may have condemned me to death, but I am better than her. I have already killed three people out of vengeance. And she is the beloved of my father and a mother to me as well." So he discarded his weapon and looked up at the sky. The Silver River[39] was tilted to the west and the moon shone faintly. "I will leave this world and spend the rest of my life in isolated mountains and forests," he decided and walked calmly to the sleeping chamber of the minister to take his leave of him. The minister heard someone outside his room, which he thought strange, so he opened the window to find Gildong there.

Gildong addressed him. "It is I, Gildong."

He then prostrated himself before the steps to the minister's room and addressed him. "I came into this life with your blood flowing through my veins, as you granted me the great favor of being born of your seed. The graciousness of the act is as boundless as the wide and deep heaven. I wanted nothing more than to spend my life repaying my father for giving me life and my mother for raising me, but an evil person within the household has conspired to make Your Lordship wary of me and to bring me harm. Fortunately, I uncovered the plot and preserved my life, but I fear that I will eventually come to an untimely end if I stay home. I must run away to save myself, so I cannot remain in Your Lordship's service any longer. I have come to take my leave of you, so I humbly wish Your Lordship good health and a long life."

The startled minister spoke. "What are you saying? What terrible thing has happened that a young boy like you would leave his home in the middle of the night to wander the world?"

Gildong remained prostrate as he replied, "You will know everything once the day dawns. Please put this unworthy son Gildong out of your mind and set your household in proper order."

The minister considered Gildong's words and thought to himself, "This child is not an ordinary person." He realized then that Gildong could not be dissuaded from his course.

The minister addressed him. "Once you leave, where will you go?"

Gildong replied, "Because of my unfortunate fate, I will become like a cloud and float about the world with no destination. I beg Your Lordship to take good care of yourself."

The minister thought in silence for a long moment before he spoke again. "You are my progeny. Even if you should leave, do not harbor an excessive ambition. Do not bring misfortune to our household by committing acts that would dishonor our ancestors. If that were to happen, our family's reputation for loyalty to the country and filial piety would come to a pitiful end. So do not bring about some calamity that I would have to witness as a white-haired old man at the end of my life."

Gildong replied in a respectful manner. "I will obey your command, but I must tell you of my sorrow that I feel deep in the marrow of my bones. I have been alive for more than ten years, and during all that time, because of my lowborn status, I have had to regard my father and older brother as my owners rather than relatives. Not once was I allowed to address my father as Father and my older brother as Brother. So how could I not be filled with grief?"

The minister let out a sigh and spoke. "If that is your greatest wish, then I will allow you to address us as such from this day on. So stay home and let go of your sorrow."

Gildong bowed down to him before he replied, "Father, please do not give any more thought to your lowly son. But, for the sake of pity, please treat my mother with kindness. That is all that I could possibly ask of you."

The minister readily agreed and spoke to him. "Since you

are determined to leave, I give you my blessing to do as you will. Take good care of yourself."

Gildong replied, "You have granted me the greatest wish of my life and you have promised to treat my mother well, so there is nothing more I desire from you. Father, I humbly beg you to live a long life with a healthy body and mind."

At the end of those words, streams of tears flowed down from his eyes and wet his clothes. As he then left his father's quarters, closing the door behind him, the minister felt a great compassion for him. But the minister was also filled with anxiety at the thought of what may have occurred that night that caused him to leave.

Gildong went into his mother's chamber to bid her farewell. "I must flee in exile, on a long and rough road that stretches endlessly before me. I ask you, Mother, not to worry about your unworthy son and to take good care of yourself as you await my return."

Gildong's mother grabbed her son's hands and wept as she spoke to him. "I wanted you to grow up to become a person of importance, so I prayed night and day that you would one day find the opportunity to strengthen our family. But then I could do nothing but watch as Chorang deceived His Lordship. How desolate my life became then. What has happened now that you must abandon me to my solitude? Once you leave, there is no telling when we will see each other again. If you must go, then go. But return to me as soon as possible for the sake of my love for you."

As Gildong bowed down twice and took his final leave of her, he could hardly speak for the emotions that overwhelmed him. As the golden rooster crowed with the coming of the new day and sunlight came blazing from the east, there were no more words that could be uttered to express the love between mother and son. Their inevitable parting was drenched in tears.

Gildong stepped out of the house and gazed upon clouds and mountains raised in layers upon layers and a great body of water stretched out through the land. He realized that he was now a wanderer without a master, who would travel aimlessly with no destination, and he thought how lost a single individual was in the immensity of the world. No matter how hard he tried to suppress his feelings, he was overcome with grief at not knowing what would become of him.

Meanwhile, Chorang became concerned when no news came after she had sent the assassin to Gildong's sleeping chamber, so she dispatched a loyal maid to spy upon the cottage. She returned after a while and informed her, "The noble son is nowhere to be found, but there are three headless corpses lying about in the room."

Shocked by the report, Chorang went to the inner chamber and told the minister's wife of what her maid had seen. The minister's wife became terrified, so she summoned her son and related the news. He went out and searched for Gildong but could find no trace of him.

He went to the minister in great trepidation and informed him, "Gildong murdered people in the night and ran away."

The astounded minister spoke out. "Gildong came to me last night and took leave of me with great sorrow. It was all because of this."

The assistant section chief dared not conceal things from his father any longer, so he told him the truth of what had happened. "Because Gildong was causing you worry, to the extent of making you ill, I considered various ways to allay your anxiety. When I consulted Chorang about the matter, she suggested that we hire an assassin to quietly get rid of Gildong. She thought that would avert future disaster and restore you to health. That is what led to Gildong committing this serious act and leaving home."

The minister heard him out before scolding him. "With such a simple mind, how could you serve at the royal court?" He spoke out in anger. "My fury can only be relieved by seeing Chorang dragged out of the inner chamber and killed."

And so he ordered. "Go get Chorang right now and execute her." But then he stopped to think. "What if people hear of what transpired? Gildong's mother might be blamed for the murders and receive punishment. It would be best to send Chorang away quietly and make her disappear."

He berated Chorang when she was brought to him. "In my rage, I was going to have you killed but I decided to banish you instead. But if you should leak a word of what happened here, I will find you and end you even if you should be a thousand *ri*[40] away. So watch yourself."

He ordered a loyal manservant to seize Chorang, take her to a faraway place, and abandon her there. He then had the dead bodies disposed of and set the household in order, firmly ordering everyone to let no word of what had occurred get out.

At the same time, after the shaman and the physiognomist who lived outside of Sungrye Gate disappeared in the night, their relatives went out searching for them but could find no trace of either. Their neighbors told them, "On that night, a great wind arose and lifted them from the ground to take them up to heaven."

And so Gildong ventured forth, sad at the thought that he could rely on no one in the world even though his parents were still alive. Because of his unfortunate fate, he wandered about like a floating cloud, making the whole world his home and finding uncomfortable rest wherever he could.

One day, he came to a land of magnificent beauty with high mountains and pristine waters. Taken by the fairness of the scenery, Gildong followed a small rocky path through the place where calm rivers flowed gently and great peaks covered with countless pine trees soared into the air. Pretty flowers and fresh grass as well as wild birds and animals all seemed to welcome him and guide him on his way. Gildong walked leisurely while enjoying the panorama, until the path ended at a sheer precipice that fell into a void, with a stream flowing down nearby. As he did not know where to go next, he was overcome by loneliness and sat down on the ground. Suddenly, a small dipping gourd appeared out of nowhere, floating down the current. He thought to himself, "This remote mountainous area is not a place where people live, so there must be a temple nearby."⁴¹ He stood up and followed the stream for a few *ri* until it ended at a waterfall, behind which he detected a hidden stone gateway.

He pushed open the portal and entered a vast land that Heaven had created in the midst of the rough terrain. Hundreds of dwellings were built close together, around a large house in the middle. Gildong went forth to the central building, where he saw numerous people enjoying a great feast with tables scattered with dishes and drinking cups. They seemed to be having an argument among themselves. This was the lair of the bandits of Taesobaek Mountain.⁴²

Gildong went up to the edge of the assembly and discreetly listened in on their conversation. He found out that they were discussing who should become their leader. He thought to himself, "After wandering about with nowhere to rest, Heaven has helped me by bringing me to this place where I will surely find the opportunity to make full use of my powers." So he walked up to the people in a proud but polite manner and bowed deeply to them in greeting.

He then addressed them. "I am Gildong, the son of High Minister Hong of Gyeongseong⁴³ and his lowborn concubine. I could not countenance being treated as an inferior in the household, so I left voluntarily to wander aimlessly about the world, resting wherever I could. Now Heaven has decreed that I should come upon this place. Proud men, I ask you to disregard the youthfulness of my appearance and test my qualities so that you may see that I am worthy to live among you and to share everything with you."

Everyone stared at Gildong in silence for a while.

At last one of them spoke out. "You have the appearance of a heroic personage. So I will tell you of two tasks that you can take on to demonstrate your worth to us. First, over there is a rock called Sobu Stone, which is a thing of a thousand *geun*.⁴⁴ If you can lift it, then we will know your strength. Second, we want to attack Haein Temple in Hapcheon County⁴⁵ and steal its treasures. Thousands of monks live there. A great deal of wealth could be gained, but we have not been able to come up with a good plan. If you should achieve both goals, we will make you our leader and share everything with you."

Gildong, greatly pleased, replied, "Born as a true man, I have studied the stars above and the ways of *eum* and *yang*[46] as well as the *Military Rules* of Sonja and Oja.[47] I have also mastered the magical powers of invisibility and metamorphosis. If I could have become the commander of three armies,[48] I would surely have risen to the rank of a great general in a time of war or a high minister in a time of peace, to have my portrait hung at Girin House[49] and my name renowned for a thousand years. For such is the destiny of a great man. But I was subject to a misfortune and my fate turned out to be a harsh one, so I could not participate in the affairs of the world. I became filled with frustration all my life. Given such difficulties I have had to face, the two tasks you have put before me are nothing."

The men were pleased by his words and spoke to him. "If all that is so, we will test you as you wish."

They led him to the spot where Sobu Stone lay. Gildong folded up his sleeves, picked up the rock, and took several steps before he threw it in the air.

As he then walked proudly back to the bandits, they talked excitedly among themselves. "That is one powerful man. None among thousands of us could lift that rock, yet today he came and threw it in the air. How can we not be pleased that Heaven has helped us by sending him to us to be our leader?"

They sat Gildong on a high seat and offered him cups of spirits they poured for him. They then presented themselves to him officially, bringing him a sealed book that listed their names in rows, and another that gave a full account of their possessions and supplies. After Gildong perused the texts, he ordered a white horse to be sacrificed and drank its blood.

He swore an oath before all the men. "From this moment on, we will combine all of our strength and never abandon one another, even in a time of disaster. And so we will stay together for all time without ever forgetting one another. But if any of you should betray us or disobey me, you will be dealt with through military law."

All responded as one. "We soldiers would not dare go against the command of our general."

Gildong was satisfied and enjoyed himself throughout the feasting.

From that day on, Gildong participated with the multitude in practicing horsemanship, archery, and swordsmanship. Within a month, discipline became firmly established in the ranks of the soldiers, who constantly and rigorously practiced their martial skills.

One day Gildong brought everyone together and addressed them. "Soon I plan to have us attack Haein Temple in Hapcheon County. Anyone who goes against any of my commands as I unfold my stratagem will be subjected to military justice."

Everyone prostrated themselves before him in gratitude.

Gildong picked a sturdy donkey to ride on, then selected several tens of followers and dressed them up as the retinue of a traveling nobleman from the family of a high minister.

He spoke to all. "I will go to the temple, so wait a few days for my return."

Then he went on his way in a casual manner, looking exactly like a noble son from a high minister's household. Everyone praised him profusely for his perfect mimicry.

Gildong urged his donkey onward until he arrived at the entrance to the temple, where he sent a man ahead to announce his coming. "The son of High Minister Hong of Gyeongseong has come to study."⁵⁰

At the news, the pleased monks of the temple spoke among themselves. "How great our temple is that a high minister's progeny should visit us. A noble son from Minister Hong's family has come here to study, which could benefit us all."

Thousands of monks came out and bowed to him with their

palms pressed together in greeting. "We are grateful that you have come such a long way to be here."

Gildong replied with a serious countenance. "I have always heard that yours is a great and famous temple where the surrounding scenery is magnificent. So I have come to enjoy the view and to stay for a few months to study for the qualifying examination[51] next spring. I request that you prohibit outsiders from coming into the temple during my sojourn and prepare a quiet place for me to live in."

The monks acquiesced to his wishes with bows and began to prepare a room for him. Gildong got to his feet and looked around the main hall of the temple before he summoned a senior monk. "I will go to the government office of the neighboring town where I will stay for a few days before coming back. I ask that you ban outsiders from the temple and make my room ready while I am gone. Also, tomorrow I will order twenty *seok*[52] of white rice to be brought here, so prepare a lot of food and spirits for me when I return in the middle of this month. I will enjoy a feast with you, and start studying from that day on."

All the monks bowed to him with their palms together and praised his generosity.

Gildong then left the place quickly and returned to the bandit village, where his men happily welcomed him back.

The next day, he had the twenty *seok* of white rice sent to the temple with a notice that read as follows: "This is sent from the household of High Minister Hong to the government office with an official announcement of the gift."[53]

When the rice arrived at the temple, all the monks gladly put it in storage and prepared spirits and delicacies for the promised day of the guest's return.

Gildong summoned the bandits and addressed them. "I will head back to the temple tomorrow, where I will arrange to have all the monks restrained. Take advantage of that moment to do all that I command without fail."

The bandits assented and went forth to await his order.

When Gildong returned to Haein Temple with tens of his followers, everyone came out to wait upon him.

Gildong questioned the senior monk. "Some time ago I sent you white rice and asked that you prepare spirits and a feast. What is the status of that?"

The monk answered him. "All is ready, so we await your pleasure."

Gildong spoke. "I have heard that the scenery at the back of the temple is magnificent, and I intend to enjoy the view in your company throughout the day. So bring out every monk of this temple without leaving anyone behind."

The monks never suspected that a hidden plot was in motion. And they dared not disobey him, so they all gathered together, high and low, young and old, and went out to a green valley behind the temple. There they picked out a suitable spot and sat down in rows.

Gildong addressed them. "I will pour your drinks first."

He bade them all to drink and enjoy themselves in feasting with him, with no thought of high or low status among them. All the monks expressed their awed gratitude as they drank two or three cups of spirits. At this point, Gildong stealthily took some sand out of his sleeve and put it in his mouth before taking some food. When the monks heard a crunching sound coming from his mouth, they were shocked and began to fearfully apologize to him.

Gildong displayed great anger as he spoke out. "All I wanted was to enjoy myself with you, without distinguishing monks from laymen, yet you thought so little of me that you dared to prepare my food in such an unsatisfactory manner. How disrespectful this is."

With those words, he loudly ordered his servants to tie up all the monks. "I will go to the government office and report the reason for my action here. And then I will see about dealing with this matter with utmost seriousness."

His servants ran among the monks and bound them all up

tightly with arrowroot vines. The monks still had no idea that this was part of a plan that was now rapidly unfolding. Even with all their strength, they dared not resist as they were too disoriented by the sudden turn of events. They could only think to beg for forgiveness.

In that moment, all the bandits who had been hiding in the area received word that the monks had been restrained, so they rushed into the temple, searched out its treasures, and began to carry out the plunder as if it belonged to them. It was only then that the monks realized the trick they had fallen for, but they could hardly intervene with all their limbs tied up. They could only follow what was happening with their eyes and scream out their frustration with their mouths.

At this time, a temple servant who was carrying some dishes from a side chamber saw a horde of bandits coming into the temple and opening up its storehouse to transport its goods on horses and cattle. He climbed over the temple wall and ran to the town of Hapcheon, where he reported to the local magistrate that hundreds of outlaws were stealing the temple's property. The startled magistrate mobilized all the servants and citizens of the town, old and young, and ordered them to catch the criminals at Haein Temple.

The bandits finished loading all the treasures on horses and cattle and were about to head for a narrow mountainside path when Gildong spoke to them. "Take the big road to the south, and do not worry about it."

His men spoke out in dismay. "We fear that government soldiers will catch us there when they arrive, as they soon will."

Gildong laughed out loud and replied, "You are like little children who could not possibly understand my deep stratagem. Have no fear. Once you go out the temple's entrance, take the big road south. I will make sure that the approaching soldiers head north."

After the bandits heard him out, they all rushed down the big road southward. Gildong returned to the temple, where he put on the robe and hat of a monk and climbed on top of a high hill. From there, he could see thick dust raised by a multitude of soldiers who were approaching like a great wind while shaking heaven and earth with the noises of their drums, horns, and war cries.

Gildong shouted at them, "Soldiers, do not head south, for the bandits have gone north. Go after them on the northward path to catch them."

He lifted the sleeve of his robe and pointed toward the small path. The soldiers heard the monk's words, saw him indicate northward, and followed his direction.

Gildong left the hill only then to guide the bandits on. Once they were on their way, he discreetly used his magic to transport himself to their lair, where he ordered the bandits who had stayed behind to go and welcome their returning comrades.

After a time, they all arrived with thousands of horses and cattle, and they all prostrated themselves before Gildong to give him thanks. "General, not even a supernatural spirit could fathom your strange magic and marvelous powers."

Gildong laughed and replied, "As a true man making his way in the world, I would not have dared to take on the position of your leader if I did not possess such talents."

He then commanded spirits and food to be brought and invited the men to partake in them, which brought them much joy. The next day, he organized a great feast, after which they took account of all the treasures they had stolen, which turned out to be enormous in value. He then distributed rewards to his men and created the name of Hwalbindang⁵⁴ for their village.

He addressed all the bandits. "We will go forth across the eight provinces of Joseon⁵⁵ and seize wealth that was ill-gotten, but we will also help the impoverished and the oppressed by giving them goods. And we will do so without ever revealing our identities. We will go after the powerful who obtained their riches by squeezing the common people and take away their unjustly gained possessions."

At this time, the soldiers of Hapcheon County traveled for tens of *ri* through the northward path in search of the outlaws, but they could find no trace of them. When they realized that there was nothing they could do, they returned to the government office and informed the astonished magistrate of their failure.

The magistrate sent a report to the office of the provincial governor. "Hundreds of criminals came out of nowhere and attacked Haein Temple in broad daylight and took away all its treasures. I sent out soldiers, but they could not find them. I am reporting this news to request that you dispatch the police to apprehend them."

The provincial governor was startled by the report, so he forwarded it to the king himself, who became worried and sent out a pronouncement across the eight provinces. "Whether you are a nobleman or a commoner, if you catch these outlaws I will reward you with great wealth and make you the lord of ten thousand households."

The pronouncement created a great stir as all those who read it aspired to catch the criminals.

One day, Gildong summoned his men and addressed them. "Whatever happens, we must not forget that we are still people of this country. When the time comes, we will do whatever is necessary to demonstrate our loyalty. We may be outlaws living in a mountainside hideout, but we will not commit acts of treason by stealing the property of the common people or inflicting harm on them. Nor will we take treasures being sent to the capital or money and grain being collected by the government.[56] From now on, all members of Hwalbindang[57] will abide by our great laws, and those of you who engage in unrighteous deeds will be dealt with through military law. So make sure none of you bring such guilt upon yourself."

All the bandits acquiesced to his command as one.

Several months passed before Gildong summoned them again. "Now that our storehouse is empty, I mean for us to go to the administrative center of Hamgyeong Province[58] and take the grain and arms out of its warehouse. Travel there individually, steal discreetly into the citadel, and hide within until a fire is set outside the south gate. When the governor, his officials, and other people leave the citadel to deal with the fire, take advantage of their absence to locate the grain and arms and carry them out. But do not touch a single piece of property that belongs to the common people."

Then Gildong and sixty of his men went forth, dressed in disguises. On the third watch[59] of an appointed night, he went to the south gate of the citadel and ordered his men to gather dry straw and make a massive pile. They then set it on fire. As light from the flames soared into the sky, people rushed about in agitation, not knowing what to do.

At this moment Gildong went to the governor's hall and shouted out, "The royal tomb[60] is on fire. The officials and guards there have all perished, so I bid you to put out the fire quickly."

When the governor was awakened by those words, he became terrified. He hurriedly got up and saw the firelight reach the sky, so he summoned all the servants and everyone else in the citadel, men and women, young and old, and led them to the tomb, leaving not a single guard at the storehouse. Gildong led his men as they opened up the building, loaded the grain onto horses and cattle, and left through the north gate of the citadel. He then used his magic to decrease the distance between them and their village, so that after riding all night they reached their destination just as light dawned in the east.

Gildong addressed the bandits. "We have committed a criminal act that will be reported to the capital, so they will surely come after us. I worry that when they fail to catch us, innocent people will be blamed and executed. If that were to happen, we would be responsible. To prevent such a course, I will write up a notice that reads 'The grain and arms in the storehouse were stolen by Hong Gildong, the leader of Hwalbindang,' and display it on the gate of the Hamgyeong Province administrative center."

All the bandits were shocked to hear those words. "General, why would you invite misfortune upon yourself?"

Gildong laughed and replied, "Do not worry, my soldiers. I have a plan to evade capture, of course. So stop arguing and do as I command."

The bandits' concern was not allayed, but they dared not disobey him. They took the notice he had written and waited until darkness fell before they put it up on the gate. That night, Gildong fashioned eight human figures out of straw and cast a magic spell that imbued each of them with a spirit. At once, the eight straw men sprouted arms and began talking loudly as they transformed themselves into eight Gildongs. As they joined their maker in speaking chaotically among themselves, none could tell which among the nine was the true Gildong.

All the bandits laughed and applauded. "The general possesses marvelous magical skills that not even a supernatural spirit could fathom."

Gildong gave each of the eight straw Gildongs five hundred men to command and ordered them to go forth to the eight provinces. After they fitted themselves with traveling clothes and equipment and went on their way, Gildong lay down to rest at Hwalbindang. The straw men themselves could not tell which among them was the true Gildong.

Meanwhile, the governor of Hamgyeong Province returned from putting out the fire and was met by a soldier in charge of guarding the storehouse, who hurriedly reported to him, "While the citadel was empty, thieves took all the grain and arms in the storehouse and left."

The astounded governor immediately mobilized his soldiers and sent them after the criminals, but there was no sign of them anywhere.

Suddenly, a soldier from the north gate reported to him. "Someone put up a notice on the gate."

The governor read it and spoke out. "There is an outlaw by the name of Hong Gildong in Hamgyeong Province. Go forth and apprehend him." He also sent a report to the central government.

The king reacted by speaking out. "I will reward whoever catches Hong Gildong."[61] And he ordered another pronouncement to be put up on all four gates of the capital: "I will grant great wealth and the lordship of ten thousand households to whoever captures Gildong."

Gildong remained at Hwalbindang while his straw men led bandits in each of the eight provinces. They traveled from one town to another, stealing gift treasures,[62] sending dirt and pebbles flying at their pursuers until they could not see or breathe, and opening up the doors of storehouses to take away grain and riches. Stories of such deeds spread quickly among the people, so that they could hardly sleep at night from anxiety.

Official reports from all eight provinces arrived at the capital. "The outlaw known as Hong Gildong transports himself by summoning a wind spirit and flying about on a cloud. He has taken treasures from high officials in every town. The situation has become extremely serious, but no one seems capable of catching him. So we beg Your Majesty to investigate this matter and see about apprehending him at last."

The king finished reading and became greatly concerned. When he reread the reports more carefully, he realized that the dates and times of the outlaw's activities were identical in all eight provinces, which worried him even more.

He let out a sigh and spoke out. "Not even the Supreme King of Cho[63] and Jegal Gongmyeong[64] could match the strength and magical powers of this bandit. What wondrous skills does he possess that he can commit these acts in all eight provinces on the same day and at the same time? This is no ordinary criminal. Who will go forth and arrest this bandit, to relieve the country of its worry and to protect its people from harm?"

Someone stepped forth from the ranks of court officials and addressed the king. "He is but an insignificant criminal. He may go about the eight provinces causing trouble with magical trickery, but this is no matter for Your Majesty to be concerned about. I may be a person of modest talents, but if you will grant me command over a company of soldiers I will capture Hong Gildong and arrest all the other bandits as well. And so I will allay our country's anxiety."

All those present before the king looked upon the speaker and saw that it was Yi Heup, Supreme General of the Police Bureau.

The king was pleased and quickly granted him hundreds of soldiers to command before addressing him. "I already know you to be a clever man, so I feel sufficiently unburdened of my worry. Take care of yourself as you go forth to apprehend the outlaw."

Yi Heup went out and instructed his soldiers to scatter and travel individually to the city of Mungyeong in Gyeongsang Province where they would rendezvous on an appointed day. He then set off on the journey himself. He traveled fifty *ri* before it began to grow dark, so he went into a tavern to rest. Suddenly, a youth dressed in a blue robe appeared, riding a donkey and accompanied by a boy servant. When the newcomer came in, the general of the police stood up and exchanged polite greetings with him before they both found places to sit. After a while, the general heard the youth let out a sigh, so he questioned him. "What troubles such a distinguished youth as yourself?"

The youth answered, "They say that all things under heaven belong to the king, and that all people are the subjects of their sovereign. I may only be a rural scholar, but I too am a loyal subject of the country."

The general spoke. "So what concerns you about our country?"

The youth replied, "An outlaw by the name of Hong Gildong is causing so much trouble across the eight provinces that high officials in every town can hardly sleep. The king has become so worried that he has sent word everywhere that he will grant an important post to anyone who captures the outlaw. I am too weak to do so by myself, and it saddens me that I cannot find someone to aid me on this quest."

The general addressed him. "You have a valiant spirit and appearance, and you speak in an upright manner. I am a person of little talent, but I want to give you whatever help I can. The two of us should collaborate to achieve the goal of apprehending the criminal and so relieve the country of its worry."

The youth replied, "They say that the bandit possesses superhuman courage as well as the strength of many men, so we should combine our forces to catch him. Or else much harm could come to us."

The general spoke. "As true men, once we swear loyalty to each other we can never go back on it, even in the face of death."

The youth addressed him. "I have been trying to catch that criminal by myself, unable to find a courageous man to work with, so I have been feeling dejected. But now that I have met you, I am no longer concerned. I wish to test your strength, so please follow me."

The youth led the general to a place where there was a lofty rock and they climbed up to its top.

He sat down and spoke to the general. "Kick me with full force, so that I may know your strength."

As the general stared at the youth sitting on the edge of the rock, he thought to himself, "Even if this youth possesses the power to move a mountain, he will surely tumble down if I kick him." And so he hit him with both legs, using all his strength.

But the youth merely moved his body to one side and spoke. "You are truly a mighty man. I have tested many people already, but none could move me from my position. But after you kicked me I could feel my organs vibrate and my body shiver, so I know that you are a man of tremendous power. There is no question that the two of us will catch Gildong. If you follow me again we are bound to succeed at the task. So come."

The youth led him up to a place of many mountains. The general followed until he found himself in a rough terrain full of thickly growing trees, where he lost all sense of direction.

The youth spoke to him. "Over there is Gildong's lair. I will go in first and find out the enemy's strength, so wait here for me."

The startled general objected. "We agreed to face life and death together before we came here, so why would you leave me alone when there are wolves about?"

The youth laughed and addressed him. "How could a true man like you be afraid of mere wolves? If you are truly frightened, go in yourself and I will wait for you."

The general replied, "I like the confident way you speak. Go ahead and take account of the enemy's strength quickly. Do not forget that we will achieve greatness if we succeed at this."

The youth smiled at him without responding and went swiftly into the mountain, leaving the general alone. As the sun set and the moon rose in the east, wolves appeared in all directions. The general became increasingly fearful, yet he could do nothing but embrace a large tree and wait for the youth to return. Suddenly, deafening noises reverberated through the air and tens of soldiers appeared, descending from the mountain. The general regarded them with terror as he saw that they were men of fearsome appearance. He tried to flee but soon found himself surrounded on all sides.

The soldiers addressed him. "Are you Yi Heup, the Supreme General of the Police Bureau? We were ordered by our general to capture you, so we were wandering about looking for you. But we did not expect to run into you here."

They put him in chains and led him forward like the wind so that he could hear nothing but the sound of air passing by. Forced to run for tens of *ri* until they arrived at a stone gate, the general was utterly disoriented by his sudden fall into danger. Beyond the gate, he was taken through a vast land where sunlight shone, a place that had the appearance of a supernatural realm beyond the world of the living.

He thought to himself, "I have been captured by men who came out of nowhere and brought me to this strange place, so what hope do I have of getting out alive?" When he managed to regain some of his composure, he looked around and saw a beautiful palace illuminated by a serene light. Countless soldiers wearing yellow caps stood about in a dignified manner with serious expressions on their faces. The general could not tell whether he was present there in his body, or if he had died and it was only his soul that was in the wondrous world. Suddenly, a loud sound issued before him. Many soldiers grabbed him and made him kneel before a high throne. The general could do nothing but stay still and await his fate.

From the palace, a great king dressed in a silk robe and a jade belt appeared and sat on the throne before reprimanding him loudly. "How dare such a small and insignificant person as you presume to go after General Hong? You have aroused the fury of the mountain spirits of the eight provinces, who have ordered, 'Send the wretch to the Palace of the Ten Kings,[65] where he will be indicted for his crimes and cast into the underworld. He has deceived his monarch with his nonsense, so he must pay for the transgression and his progeny must be kept under watch.' So off to the underworld with you." The king ordered those around him, "Take this criminal and imprison him in the underworld."

Tens of soldiers rushed to obey his command and began to bind the general as he pleaded, "I am but an insignificant person who has been condemned even though I am innocent of any crime. So I beg you on my hands and knees to spare me from the underworld." He began to weep. Those around him laughed with their mouths covered.

Another admonition came from the king. "You silly man, how can the Mansion of the Underworld, the Palace of the Ten Kings, and the House of Darkness[66] exist in this world? Lift up your head and look at me. I am none other than Hong Gildong, the leader of Hwalbindang. In your ignorance, you thought presumptuously that you were capable of catching me. So I decided to test your strength by appearing to you yesterday as a youth in a blue robe. And then I brought you here."

He ordered the general's restraints to be undone and invited him into the palace, where he sat him down and offered him spirits. "Ten thousand of the likes of you could not possibly capture me. I could kill you so that you would not see the world again, but there is no reason for me to harm such a lowly person as you. I will also let you live because you were acting under the king's order. But I will punish you if you tell anyone that you saw me. Do not speak of what you have experienced here, and appreciate the favor I am granting you by sparing your life. If you should encounter anyone who speaks ill of me, warn that person of his folly lest he also fall for my trickery."

Three more people who had been captured were brought to the stairs of the palace and made to kneel.

Gildong reprimanded them. "Listen to me well. You blindly followed Yi Heup in trying to apprehend me. I could kill you all as a warning to others as foolish as you. But since I have already decided to spare your leader, I will do the same for you. I will let you live, but if you should ever act beyond your station again, I will find you and kill you without even moving from my seat. Do not forget this, and act sensibly from now on." And he ordered his men to release the three captives from their restraints as well.

He offered them all spirits before consoling the general. "I give you this cup of spirits as a sign of my affection for you."

It was only then that the general, moving himself to sit properly before Gildong, managed to gather his wits enough to see that he had been with the youth in the blue robe all along. As he finally realized how he had been fooled so thoroughly, he put his head down and could not say a word. He dared not refuse the spirits offered by Gildong, so he took them until he became drunk. As Gildong talked to him in a pleasant manner, the general could only marvel at his powers.

After a while, the general was suddenly awakened from his drunken state and felt a terrible thirst. He tried to get up but could not move his limbs. Puzzled by his strange predicament, he looked up and saw a tree with three leather sacks hanging horizontally from it. He opened them one by one and found the servants he had taken with him when he had left Gyeongseong.

"Am I dreaming or awake?" he said. "Did I die and go to the afterworld, or am I still in the living world? I was headed for Mungyeong to rendezvous with my men, but somehow I ended up in this place."

He then looked around and realized that he was on top of Bugak Mountain[67] in Jangan. As he could do nothing but wonder how he got there, it felt like he was lost in a springtime dream.

He addressed his servants. "I followed a youth in a blue robe, only to end up here. How did you get captured?"

The three servants replied, "We were sleeping at the tavern when there was a thunderclap, and a tempest enveloped us and took us far away. We had no idea where we were going, and we would never have guessed that we would end up here."

The general spoke to them. "Everything that happened is so fantastic that we would hardly be believed if we told anyone about it. And we may end up being punished for it, so do not speak of these things. There is no doubt that even a supernatural spirit could not fathom Gildong's marvelous talents and uncanny powers. How could ordinary people hope to catch him? If we return to the city now we will surely be punished, so let us wait a few months before we go back."

The order from the government to capture the outlaw went across the eight provinces, yet none could overcome Gildong's unlimited ability to transform himself. On the great roads of Jangan, he rode around on a one-wheeled cart[68] as it pleased him, yet none thought to catch him. And in small towns he went about on a two-horse litter[69] and left public notices, yet none knew his true identity. He also toured the eight provinces, and if he came across a corrupt official, he appeared in the guise of a government inspector[70] and executed the unjust before sending a letter to the king, which read as follows: "Your subject Hong Gildong makes a hundred obeisances to Your Majesty. I report that during my tour of the eight provinces, whenever I came across a corrupt official who acted with injustice, who stole the property of the common people, and who lacked benevolence, I have executed him for his crimes."

The king read the letters and spoke out in anger. "This wretch goes about committing such acts in every town. What is to be done about this?"

Reports from provincial governors continued to carry such news, so the monarch's concern multiplied. "Where did this wretch come from?" he asked.

No one in the court seemed to know the answer at first, but then someone finally stepped out of the ranks of officials and spoke out. "I have heard that Hong Gildong is the son of the former state councilor of the right[71] Hong *mo*, and the younger half brother of Hong Inhyeon, who is currently the third minister[72] at the Ministry of Personnel. I have also heard that he committed murder in the household before he left home. Your Majesty should summon Hong *mo* to court and question him."

The king listened and spoke out. "How is it that you knew this but did not tell me right away?" He then immediately ordered the Office for the Deliberation of Forbidden Affairs[73] to dispatch an inspector to apprehend Hong *mo* and Inhyeon.

The official, accompanied by policemen, entered Minister Hong's house and relayed the order, causing turmoil among the family members. The minister and his son submitted themselves to the royal command and followed the officers to their headquarters.

When the inspector reported the arrest to the king, the monarch sat on his throne at Injeong Hall[74] and ordered Hong *mo* to be brought before him to be reprimanded. "I hear that the outlaw Hong Gildong is your son. As someone who worked for the country as a high-ranking statesman, you must have heard stories of his deeds. Even before I sent out the order to capture him, you should have taken it upon yourself to bring him in and so relieve the country of its worry. Yet you and your son pretended to know nothing. How can you call yourself a statesman of principle?" He then stripped the minister of his title and put him in prison.

Afterward, he ordered Inhyeon to be brought before him. "I hear that Gildong is your half brother. If you want to prevent calamity from falling upon your family, go and apprehend him quickly."

Inhyeon prostrated himself with his brow on the ground and spoke. "Ever since my lowborn brother murdered people and left home in exile out of disloyalty and lack of filial piety, we had no news of him for many years. We did not even know if he was alive or dead. My aged father has fallen ill because of this, and he is now on the verge of death. I have learned that Gildong has committed crimes against the country and is deserving of death, so it is just that my father and I should be executed ten thousand times. But I beg Your Majesty to reconsider this matter and please spare my father the punishment for the crimes committed by his son. Grant him mercy and I swear to bring Gildong before you, even if I should lose my life in the effort."

As he made obeisance to the king countless times, the monarch was impressed by his filial piety as well as his eloquence. So he had Hong *mo* released and reappointed him as state councilor of the right. He then granted the third minister[75] the governorship of Gyeongsang Province and gave him a year to apprehend Gildong. Inhyeon bowed deeply in gratitude before taking leave of his sovereign. He went home, bade farewell to his parents, and left to take up his new position.

After traveling for about ten days, he arrived at the provincial center of Gyeongsang. There, he composed a notice and sent it out to every town. It read as follows: "Once a person is born into this world, it is essential to abide by the five relationships.[76] And at the center of the five relationships are the king and the father. To disobey a king or a father is an act of disloyalty and an abandonment of filial piety, for which there can be no forgiveness. Because of your actions, our father, in his gray-haired old age, has become a criminal in the eyes of the country, and so there is no end to his tears. His Majesty, in his fury, imprisoned him but granted me the position of governor so that I may bring you in. If I should fail to carry out His Majesty's order, then all the illustrious achievements of our ancestors will come to nothing as our entire family is destroyed. Would that not be a tragedy? Gildong, I ask you to think of the welfare of your older brother and father and surrender yourself quickly so that you can prevent calamity from falling upon our household and ill repute upon a hundred generations of the Hong." He had the notice transcribed and posted everywhere.

Meanwhile, Gildong ordered the false Gildongs to send

their soldiers back to Hwalbindang and surrender themselves at the administrative center of each province. The governor,[77] after he dispatched the notice, naturally found himself beset by anxiety, so he suspended all public works and spent his days in a melancholy state.

One day, he heard a great noise from the south gate, and a soldier reported to him. "A youth on a donkey has come with tens of servants at the outer gate. He begs an audience with Your Lordship."

The governor thought that strange, so he ordered the east side gate to be opened. "I don't know such a person. Who could it be?"

The youth came forth riding his donkey in a dignified manner and went up to the governor's seat to present himself. The governor did not recognize him at first, but after looking carefully at him for some time he realized that it was none other than Gildong. He dismissed everyone around him before taking hold of Gildong's hands.

He wept as he spoke. "Ever since you left our household and disappeared without a trace, our father could hardly eat or sleep because of you. He has been much reduced in health because of his sorrow and worry over you. Yet you have acted without filial piety, leading outlaws and causing trouble in our peaceful land, all because of your dissolute nature. His Majesty, in his wrath, has ordered me to arrest you, and made me the governor here so I can fulfill his command. If I should fail to do so, I will surely receive the punishment due to a traitor, so what can be done about this? As the old saying goes, 'One can avoid a calamity sent down by Heaven, but there is no escape from a misfortune one has brought down upon oneself.' So think on this deeply and go to Gyeongsa[78] to face the judgment of Heaven. If you do not, then our entire family will be destroyed." As he finished speaking, tears flowed down his cheeks like rain.

Gildong bowed his head and spoke quietly. "I have come because I heard that my brother was in danger, so I already know everything you are saying. I tell you that all this could have been prevented if only I were allowed to address my father as Father and my older brother as Brother, despite my lowborn status. But there is no use discussing what has already passed. Arrest me tomorrow and send a report of my capture to the king before dispatching me to him."

He then closed his mouth and would not answer any question he was asked.

The next day, the governor sent his report. He then put Gildong's neck and feet in cangues[79] and had him secured inside a prisoners' wagon guarded by tens of soldiers. As stories of Gildong's powers were renowned, people from every town came out to see him as he was transported through the roads.

Meanwhile, the king at Jangan was puzzled to receive reports from the governors of all eight provinces that each of them had captured Gildong. As none could tell which prisoner was the true Gildong, there was much talk of the mystery in the royal court. When soldiers from the provinces arrived with eight different Gildongs in cangues, people could not find a single thing in their appearance to tell them apart. After they were all firmly imprisoned, the king was informed of the development, which amazed him. He sat down at the Office of the Royal Secretariat[80] with his entire court to personally interrogate the prisoners.

When the soldiers of the Office for the Deliberation of Forbidden Affairs brought the eight Gildongs before him, they began to argue with one another. "You are the real Gildong, not me," they said and bickered, even falling upon one another to fight. None could tell them apart so there was much confusion.

The king spoke. "Minister Hong *mo* is sure to know the truth." And he summoned the minister. "A father knows his son. I have heard that you have one son named Gildong, but today there are eight Gildongs here, so which one is the real one? Point him out."

Upon the king's command, Minister Hong bowed down and replied, "Because of an unfortunate fate, I have come to commit an act of disloyalty toward Your Majesty, so it is fitting that I should be executed for my crimes. But even now I will do my utmost to follow the principles of a loyal official. There is a red mark on the left leg of my son Gildong, so I bid Your Majesty to order the eight to be stripped so you may look for it."

He then turned around and reprimanded the eight Gildongs. "No matter how disloyal and lacking in filial piety you are, do you not see that you are in the presence of His Majesty and your own father below him? You have caused much trouble in the world, so there can be no forgiveness for you even if you should die and become a ghost."

As soon as he finished speaking, Minister Hong vomited blood and fell in a faint, startling everyone. The king, deeply concerned, ordered his officials to save him, but none could revive him. The eight Gildongs all wept as they watched the scene. Then each of them reached into his clothes and brought out two pieces of medicine that looked like jujubes, ground them down, and put the powder into the minister's mouth. Soon the minister regained consciousness and was able to sit up.

The Gildongs spoke out. "My father achieved much wealth, honor, and glory through the favors he received from the country, so how could I dare commit immoral acts against the land? Because of some guilt I had to bear from my past life, I was born of a servant girl and was not allowed to address my own father as Father and my older brother as Brother. The frustration I felt at my station in life reached deep into the marrow of my bones. So I came to leave the world, to fulfill my ardent desire to live in a mountain forest. But then Heaven saw fit to cast me into an unseemly place where I became the leader of bandits. From the beginning, I have never stolen even the smallest portion of the country's grain or the common people's property. I did plunder treasures being sent by incompetent officials who were squeezing the common people by taking unjust amounts of their goods. They say that the king and the father are one, that just as the people partake of the bounty of the country, the child eats the food provided by the father. Your Majesty, there is no more need for you to worry anymore because I swear to you that I will leave this country within three years to explore some other land. I beg you to cancel your order to arrest me."

As soon as they finished speaking, the eight Gildongs collapsed on the ground at once. All those present were astounded and examined the inert bodies, only to discover that none of them were Gildong but only men made of straw.

The furious king struck his throne and spoke out. "Whoever proves capable of capturing Gildong quickly, I will grant him any position in the court he desires."

Since none possessed the skills to do so, they remained silent.

On the afternoon of the same day, notices appeared on all four great gates of the city that read as follows: "Hong Gildong has never been relieved of his life's frustration, so he begs His Majesty to grant his lowborn subject the position of minister of war.[81] He swears to surrender himself if he should receive the favor."

After the king read the notice, he summoned his officials to discuss it.

They remained silent at first but then spoke out. "Whatever Gildong says, he has done no great deed to merit the position. Even if he had, he should never be made minister of war since he was born of a lowly servant girl. Besides, as the order to arrest and execute him for his crimes has been sent out, it would damage the dignity of our country for him to receive his wish. Whoever finally succeeds in capturing Gildong should be given the same reward as someone who defeated an enemy country."

The king agreed and sent out such a pronouncement, yet none could get to Gildong.

The furious monarch sent a command to the governor of Gyeongsang Province. "I ordered you to bring me your lowborn brother, but all you did was make some straw men and send them off to cause further disturbance. The crimes you have to answer for have now become even more serious. From now on, do not send me fake Gildongs but only the real Gildong. That is the only way you will forestall disaster from falling upon three generations of your family."[82]

After the governor read the letter, he felt so distraught at his failure that he decided to dress up in disguise and go forth to catch Gildong himself. But that night, a youth descended from the crossbeam of his office building and bowed down to him. The governor took fright at what he first thought was a ghost, but when he looked more carefully it was none other than Gildong.

The governor regarded him strangely before rebuking him. "You wicked child. You disobeyed the king's order from above and disregarded the advice of your older brother from below. Are you trying to become an enemy of your sovereign, your father, and your brother? The whole country is in turmoil, your aged parents live in fear, and our entire family is about to be destroyed, all because of you."

Gildong laughed before he replied, "Brother, do not worry about anything. Put me in restraints and send me to Gyeongsa. But when you pick officers who will transport me to the capital, make sure that they are men who are all alone in the world, without parents or children."

The governor worried that this Gildong might be another straw man, so he checked to make sure that there was a red mark on his leg. He then ordered Gildong's limbs to be tied up before securing him in a prisoners' wagon. And he followed Gildong's instruction by selecting officers with no families and commanded them to transport the prisoner to the king in Gyeongsa with a report of his apprehension. Gildong seemed unconcerned as he drank spirits until he became inebriated.

As the party approached the capital, some of the officers went ahead to the Office of the Royal Secretariat and reported Gildong's arrest and his imminent arrival.

The king sent out a command. "Mobilize the musketeers of the Military Training Agency[83] and station them all over the place. Give them the order to shoot Gildong if he should get up."

When Gildong arrived at the Great South Gate of the capital, musketeers poured gunpowder into their weapons and surrounded him tenfold before escorting him in.

Suddenly, Gildong spoke out in a loud voice. "I have traveled all the way here in perfect comfort, so the king must know by now that I have been captured and brought to him. Hear me, you officers who escorted me to this place. I bid you not to bear ill feelings toward me even if your work should be rewarded with death."

With a single shake of his body, the chains around him fell apart like they were rotten rope, and the prisoners' wagon split open in an instant. Gildong then flew some thirty *jang* into the sky, and the musketeers around him only stared up at him in wonder, as they could not move their hands.

When the king received the report of what had happened, he spoke out in anger. "First, arrest those officers who brought Gildong here and send them away in exile."

He then discussed with his officials how best to capture Gildong. They addressed him. "Gildong has said that he will leave Joseon if he receives a royal appointment to the position of minister of war, so this may be the right time to grant him his wish."

After considering the matter, the king decided to follow this advice. He immediately sent out a notice of appointment and had it put on the Great East Gate.

Servants from the Ministry of War were sent out in search of Gildong, newly appointed as Minister Hong,[84] but they could find no trace of him. Then a youth in a blue robe and jade belt appeared, riding high on a one-wheeled cart in a casual manner.

He called out to the servants, "His Majesty, with infinite benevolence, has favored me with an appointment to the position of minister of war and has summoned me to court, so here I come."

All the servants of the ministry presented themselves to him at once. They then escorted him through roads that had been cleared for his grand procession as he went forth leisurely to present himself at the royal palace and to express his gratitude to his sovereign.

The court officials conferred among themselves and decided

to order heavily armed soldiers to lie in ambush for him outside the palace gates. "After Gildong finishes relating his appreciation to the king and comes out of the palace, pierce him with spears until he is dead." So the court officials instructed the soldiers.

When Gildong arrived at the gates, he descended from the one-wheeled cart and went up to the stone stairs before the king.

He addressed the king in a prostrate position. "I, a most disloyal and wicked subject named Hong Gildong, have committed a great crime against the country and troubled the mind of Your Majesty, so I deserve to be executed ten thousand times over. Yet Your Majesty favored me by granting a wish that relieves me of my deepest frustration in life. Your benevolence knows no bounds. I would like nothing better than to dedicate myself to repaying your kindness in what paltry way I can, but Heaven has commanded me to go elsewhere. So on this day I have come to take my leave of Your Majesty, and to wish you a long and healthy life."

After he finished speaking, he leapt into the air and went among windy clouds to float away in their midst. As he flew swiftly through them and disappeared in a single instant, none could tell where he had gone.

The king gazed up at his wake and praised him. "None throughout the ages could have matched Gildong's powers. How did I think that we could capture such a person?" He spoke further. "He is not a man deserving of death, but a grand personage."

He immediately sent out orders to the eight provinces, canceling his command to arrest Gildong. He then spoke again. "With all his talents, he would have achieved great things if he had the opportunity to serve the country with loyalty."

He could not sing Gildong's praises enough, which scandalized his officials. After Gildong took leave of the king, no report came from the provinces of any more trouble caused by him.

After Gildong bade farewell to the king, he returned to his village and summoned all the bandits to speak to them. "There is a place I need to visit briefly, so do not wander about but await my return."

On the same day, Gildong flew on a cloud in the direction of Namgyeong.[85] He came to an island country called Yul,[86] where he stopped to look around. It was a land of beautiful hills and rivers as well as an abundant population. He thought it a good place for him to seize, so he kept it in his mind as he resumed his journey. On his return trip, he visited another island and its natural sites, including a magnificent mountain called Ilbong. There he picked a fitting place for a gravesite and buried an insignia to mark its location. He toured the land and saw that it stretched six or seven hundred *ri* in every direction, with exceedingly fine waters and earth. It was a comfortable place to settle in, so Gildong thought to himself, "I will never be able to live in Joseon again, so this is a good place for me to make my new home." He then swiftly moved on.

The bandits awaited their leader for a number of months, until he suddenly appeared before them. They welcomed him and congratulated him on his safe return from such a long journey.

Gildong addressed them all. "Go to Yangcheon[87] in Yang District, and take enough material and manpower to build tens of ships there. Then, on a day of my choosing, take the ships to Seogang[88] in Gyeongseong and wait for my order. I will go to the king and obtain unhulled rice[89] from him, so make sure to meet me at the appointed time and place." And he sent them on their way.

One day, he ordered all remaining goods in the village to be gathered before he spoke to the bandits again. "Gather all your families and go to Seogang by the designated time, and wait for me." And he went forth to some unknown place.

Meanwhile, in the capital city, there had been no news of Gildong since he had taken his leave of the king. A year after he had departed, in the middle of the ninth lunar month, on a night when a fresh and chilly wind blew and the moon shone brightly, the king wanted to enjoy the moonlight, so he wandered about the back garden accompanied by tens of eunuchs.[90]

Suddenly, a youth descended from the clouds and prostrated himself at the palace stairs before the king.

The startled monarch spoke out. "A heavenly official has descended from Heaven to our human world, so I bid you to tell me your purpose in coming here."

The youth replied while remaining prostrate. "I am your former minister of war Hong Gildong."

The king addressed him in surprise. "Why do you come here in the middle of the night?"

Gildong got up and bowed to him before he replied, "All I ever wanted was to dedicate my life to serving Your Majesty. But because I was born of a lowly servant girl, no matter how much I increased my talents by mastering the *Six Teachings* and the *Three Summaries*[91] and aspired to pass the military examinations through my prowess in archery, I could never join the ranks of military officers. And even after I mastered the *Four Books*, the *Five Classics*,[92] and other ancient classics in the hope of passing the civil examinations, I could not work at the Office of Special Councilors.[93] So I abandoned the affairs of the world and wandered about for a while, until I came to commit unseemly acts with a group of men. I have caused trouble for the kingdom and brought dishonor to my ancestors. Yet Your Majesty, through your infinite benevolence, saw fit to pardon me and to release me from my life's frustration. My desire is to dedicate my life to serving you with the loyalty of Yong Bong and Bigan,[94] to pay you back in what paltry way I can for your favor. But I know that the court would never accept me because of my lowborn status, and the world would never forget that my name is associated with banditry. It grieves me to take my leave of Your Majesty before I depart from Joseon. And I beg Your Majesty to unleash your benevolence once more and grant me three thousand *seok* of unhulled rice, and have it transported to Seogang. By doing so, you will preserve the lives of thousands of people."

The king considered his words for a while before he addressed him. "I will grant you the three thousand *seok* of rice as you desire, but how do you plan to transport them?"

Gildong bowed as he replied, "I have made arrangements to do so, so I beg Your Majesty not to concern yourself about that."

The king spoke. "I have never looked you in the face before, so lift up your head to me."

Gildong obeyed but with his eyes closed, so the king questioned him. "Why do you not open your eyes?"

Gildong replied, "I am afraid that Your Majesty might take fright, so I dare not."[95]

The king could not command him otherwise, so he dismissed him. Gildong bowed to him again. "Your Majesty has granted me three thousand *seok* of rice out of your infinite benevolence, so I bid you to live a long and healthy life."

After he finished speaking, Gildong leapt into the air and flew on a fierce and suddenly rising wind. He played a jade flute as he made his way through white clouds. The king thought Gildong's powers very wondrous.

On the following day, the monarch sent out an order to the officials at the Office for Dispensing Benevolence.[96] "Take three thousand *seok* of unhulled rice and pile it up at Seogang."

The officials immediately gathered servants and had them transport the grain to Seogang, where it was piled up like a hill. Suddenly, tens of ships appeared, and men, women, and children, all together six or seven thousand people, disembarked to carry the rice aboard. The people of Seogang and the servants from the Office for Dispensing Benevolence did not know what was going on, so they questioned the sailors, who answered, "The king has granted this rice to Lord Neunghyeon."[97]

Once all the rice was loaded, Gildong bowed four times in the direction of Jangan and spoke out. "The former minister of war Hong Gildong has received the favor of His Majesty. These three thousand *seok* of rice will preserve the lives of thousands, so His Majesty's benevolence knows no bounds." And they sailed leisurely forth.

The astonished officials of the Office for Dispensing Benevolence reported the event to the king, who laughed and spoke. "I granted the rice to Gildong, so do not concern yourself about it."

None of his officials could understand what had transpired.

Gildong and his three thousand bandits, along with their families, possessions, useful tools, and the three thousand *seok* of rice, left Joseon on ships and sailed out to the endless ocean with their masts to the wind. They eventually arrived safely at an island called Jae[98] near Namgyeong, where they built dwellings, worked the land, and traded with the merchants of Namgyeong. They also accumulated a great deal of weapons and gunpowder, and practiced military discipline.

One day Gildong summoned the bandits and addressed them. "I need to go to Mangdang Mountain[99] so I can obtain a drug to use on an arrowhead.[100] Guard the island well while I am gone and await my return."

They requested that he return to them quickly. Gildong bade farewell to his men and crossed the sea to the land beyond, reaching Mangdang Mountain in a matter of days.

At this time, in the county of Nakcheon[101] there was a rich man whose family name was Bek and whose personal name was Yong. He had a daughter of such beauty that the moon hid itself and flowers became embarrassed before her fairness. She had also mastered the *Classic of Poetry*, the *Classic of History*, and other ancient classics.[102] She was greatly beloved by her parents, who sought a scholar with the luminous appearance of Du Mokji and the literary talent of Yi Jeokseon.[103] They hoped to find such a person with whom their daughter could enjoy the blissful union of the phoenix.[104] Yet no man of such qualities appeared, so the couple often sighed in concern after their child reached the age of eighteen.

One day, a sudden wind blew with such ferocity that people could not distinguish between heaven and earth. When the day finally became calm and bright, Bek Yong and his wife discovered that their daughter had disappeared. The distraught couple searched everywhere but no trace of her could be found. They could hardly eat or drink from grief as they spent all their time wandering the streets and speaking out. "Whoever finds our daughter, we will accept as our son-in-law and reward him with great wealth." And they went about weeping in sadness.

At this time, Gildong was traveling through Mangdang Mountain, digging up plants to use as medicine, when he suddenly realized that the sun had set behind the western mountains and birds had gone deep into the forest to sleep. The pathway he had come upon was buried in darkness, so he wandered aimlessly about the top of the mountain. After a while, he heard the voices of people talking loudly and saw fire in the distance, so he felt relieved and made his way to the sound and the light. When he came close, however, he realized that the noise was made not by humans but by hundreds of monsters. They were enjoying themselves during a break in their journey, after they had kidnapped a woman. Gildong observed them carefully and saw that while they had the appearance of human beings, they were in fact beastly creatures called *uldong* who had been living in the mountain for a long time, using the magical power of metamorphosis to look like people. Gildong thought to himself, "I have done much traveling across the world and seen many things, but I have never encountered such creatures before. They are a strange sight to behold. They have also taken a woman captive, so I should kill them and save her."

He hid himself well before he shot one of them with an arrow. The creature made a great noise before he fled with his many soldiers. Gildong chased after them, but the place was unfamiliar to him so he could not find his way in the night. Feeling sad that he had failed to rescue the woman, he spent the night in the woods. The next day, he was on his way down the mountain when he found traces of blood shed by the monster. He followed the trail for several *ri*, until he came upon a great building made of stone.

Gildong went up to its stone gate, where an *uldong* who stood guard there questioned him. "What kind of a person are you that you would venture so deep into the mountain?"

Gildong looked at him and saw that he was one of the monsters he had seen in the night. He was secretly pleased as he thought to himself, "Let us see how all this plays out."

And he spoke out. "I am a man from Joseon who makes his living by practicing the healing arts. I came up here to obtain some medicine, but then, to my embarrassment, I lost my way. I bid you to tell me the right direction to go."

When the creature heard those words, he questioned him further. "You say that you practice the healing arts. Can you heal a wound?"

Gildong replied, "I possess the medical skills of Hwa Ta and Pyeon Jak,[105] so a mere wound is nothing to me."

The joyful creature spoke out. "Heaven has sent you to us to help our great king."

Gildong pretended not to understand and questioned him. "What do you speak of? Tell me your story."

The *uldong* informed him. "Our great king has obtained a new wife for himself, but on our way back home an arrow came flying out of nowhere and pierced him. Not only could he not consummate his marriage last night, but the state of his health is in a precarious condition. Come and use your good medicine to let your healing skills shine forth," he said and quickly went inside.

He returned after a while, asked Gildong to follow him, and led him to a palace within. Inside, there was a throne surrounded by fresh grass and beautiful flowers in full bloom. An *uldong* lay there moaning in pain. Gildong looked around and saw a woman in the stone building who was trying to commit suicide by hanging herself from a crossbeam. Two other women were holding on to her steadfastly, preventing her from carrying out her intent. Gildong recognized the first woman as the one from the previous night.

Gildong went before the king and spoke deceitfully to him. "I can see that your illness is not a serious one. I carry in my pocket a miracle medicine that needs to be stirred into liquid. If you take it, the poison inside your body will dissipate and new flesh will appear. With just one dose, not only will your wound heal, but you will also attain immortality, great king."

The *uldong* was filled with joy at those words and spoke out. "I did not think to take precaution against a misfortune like this falling on me, and my illness has taken me to the verge of death. How I lamented this fateful turn in my life. But you have come to me by the grace of Heaven, so now I can hope to recover my health. I beg you to use your good medicine to save me."

Gildong immediately took a package of drug out of his pocket, diluted it in liquid, and fed it to the creature. After a while, the *uldong* began hitting himself in the stomach as he screamed out in pain.

He spoke to Gildong. "We have never had cause to become enemies, so why did you feed me a poisonous drug to kill me?"

He then summoned all the *uldongs* and addressed them. "Out of nowhere, this wicked person has appeared in my life's path, and he has murdered me. I order you to avenge my death by killing him." As soon as he finished speaking, he fell down dead.

All the *uldongs* wailed in grief as they took up their swords and rebuked Gildong. "Foul enemy, who has harmed our king and caused his death, receive the blows of our swords." And they charged him.

Gildong laughed out loud and talked back to them. "I did not kill your king. He has just lived out his natural span of life."

As the enraged *uldongs* came at him, he wanted to fight them, but he had no weapon in hand to defend himself with. In the dire situation, Gildong flew up into the air to flee, but the *uldongs* were crafty monsters who had been practicing magic for thousands of years. As he aroused a tempest to make his escape, the creatures let out a noise in unison that brought them a wind that they rode in pursuit. Left with no other choice, Gildong cast a spell that summoned Heavenly Soldiers who descended from above and restrained all the *uldongs*. The monsters were brought down and forced to kneel before the stairs of the palace. Gildong grabbed a sword from an *uldong* and slaughtered every single one of them.

He went back inside the palace for the women he had seen before, but they began to cry and plead. "We are not monsters but humans captured by the creatures, who kept us and would not let us die. We beg you, great general, spare our lives."

Gildong considered them before he asked for their names and places of origin. One was from the family of Jeong, another of Jo, while the third was the daughter of Bek Yong of Nakcheon County. As he listened to them, he realized that they were all women from respectable families.

He immediately took them to Nakcheon County, where he found Bek Yong and explained what had happened. He then returned Bek Yong's daughter to him. He and his wife were so happy to see their child again that they organized a magnificent feast and invited all their relatives and village neighbors. After they enjoyed themselves, Bek Yong accepted Gildong as his son-in-law, sparing no expense for the grandest of weddings.

The next day, the women named Jeong and Jo asked to see Master Hong, and spoke to him with appreciation. "We were on the verge of death, but Heaven saw fit to send a great general who returned us to the world of the living. We have no wish to go anywhere without you. So we beg you, great general, not to leave us but allow us to live under your protection so that we may have the opportunity to pay you back for saving our lives."

Gildong could not resist them, so he made them his concubines.

Up to this time Gildong had not known the joys of the phoenix's union, but now that he had so suddenly gained a beautiful woman of grace and virtue as his wife, the love he felt for her knew no bounds. He took his entire family-in-law to Jae Island, where all his soldiers met him at a river's shore and congratulated him on his safe return. The men escorted the traveling party home, where they enjoyed themselves at a great feast.

Time flowed on, and three years passed since Gildong had first come to Jae Island. One night, as he took a walk to enjoy the moonlight, he gazed up at the stars and was suddenly overcome with such sorrow that he began to weep.

Lady Bek[106] questioned him. "My dear husband, in all the time I have been with you, I have never seen you sad. So what has happened on this day that you should grieve so?"

Gildong sighed as he spoke. "I am the most disloyal son in the world. There can be no forgiveness for me. I am not a native of this part of the world. I was, rather, born the son of High Minister Hong and his lowborn concubine in the country of Joseon. I could not bear to be treated as a lowly person in the household, nor could I enter into the service of the royal court. There was no way for me to realize my will and spirit as a true man, so I took leave of my parents and eventually came to live in this place. But I have constantly looked to the stars for signs of my parents' health. Just now, I saw in the constellations that my father has fallen ill and that he will soon leave this world. I am ten thousand *ri* away and I will not reach him in time. So I will never see him alive again. That is the reason for my grief."

Lady Bek also felt sad hearing his words, but she tried her best to console him. "It is hard to evade one's fate, so please do not be so distraught."

The next day, he took some men up to Ilbong Mountain and had them begin preparing a gravesite at the place he once marked.

He spoke to them. "Make the grave three *ja*[107] wide, and follow my instructions in erecting the tomb."

He then summoned his soldiers and addressed them. "On a day of my choosing, take a big ship to Seogang in Joseon and wait for my order."

He then bade farewell to Lady Bek as well as to his concubines Jeong and Jo and went forth on a small ship. On his way to Joseon, he cut off all his hair and dressed himself up as a monk.

At this time, High Minister Hong was eighty years old. He suddenly fell ill, and his condition grew serious as all medicine proved ineffective. This was in the middle of the ninth lunar month.

The minister summoned his wife and his son, the assistant section chief,[108] and addressed the latter. "I am eighty years old and I regret nothing in my life except for one thing. Gildong may have been born of a servant girl, but his talent and courage were those of an extraordinary person. He is also my progeny. Ever since he went away, I have had to live without knowing whether my own son was alive or dead. And now I will pass from this world without seeing him again. So I feel a great sorrow in my heart. After I die, take special care of Gildong's mother and make sure that she lives out her life in comfort. If Gildong should return, then lay aside the practice of separating legitimate children from the illegitimate, and act without discrimination toward him as if he were born of the same mother as you. I ask you to honor this last command from your father."

He then summoned Gildong's mother and took her hand.

He wept as he spoke to her. "The only thing I regret is that I will die without seeing Gildong again. He is not a feckless person so he will not abandon you. But, for me, I will not be able to close my eyes in peace, even after I have entered the Land of Yellow Spring."[109]

After he finished speaking, he passed away. His wife and Chunseom both fainted in grief, and the sound of wailing reverberated throughout the household, letting all know that the mourning period had begun.[110] After the family members regained their composure, they made certain that all the rites were performed with the utmost care. They put on their funeral clothes and kept watch over the coffin in the house.

At this time, a male servant and a female one came and spoke to them. "A monk has come asking to offer condolences before the monumental tablet[111] of the deceased." The mourning son[112] thought it peculiar but allowed the visitor to come.

The monk entered the house in a respectful manner, went up to the minister's monumental tablet, and began to wail in grief.

The household servants spoke among themselves. "His Lordship was never close to any monk, so who is he that he should mourn so sadly?" They thought the scene peculiar.

Some time passed before Gildong's cries finally calmed down to sorrowful moans.

He then spoke out. "Older brother, do you not know who I am?"

Only then did the mourning son lift his head and look carefully at the monk to see that it was his younger brother, Gildong.

Filled with both joy and sadness, he cried out as he addressed him. "Heartless brother, where have you been all this time? As our father was dying, his last thoughts were of you. In his final words he said much in your favor, but he also lamented that he could not close his eyes in peace because of you."

He then took his hand and led him into the inner chamber, where the minister's wife looked upon them and spoke. "Why have you brought a monk into the inner chamber?"

The mourning son quietly replied, "This is not a stranger but my younger brother, Gildong."

The minister's wife was also filled with joy and sadness at the same time.

She addressed him. "We have received no word from you since you left us. When His Lordship's illness became serious and he began to expire, he repeatedly said that he would not be able to close his eyes in peace even in the Land of Yellow Spring because he could not see you one last time before he bade his final farewell to this world. How tragic this is."

Gildong let out a sigh and replied, "This disloyal son Gildong lost all desire to live in the world, so I went into a mountain and cut off all my hair to become a monk. I then studied geomancy[113] and found a suitable gravesite for my parents to rest in after their passing. At least in that way I sought to repay my parents for the immense gift of life they have given me, and to make up what paltry amount I can for my lack of filial piety."

The minister's wife sent a maid to summon Gildong's mother. When Chunseom heard that Gildong had come, she lost all composure and fainted. The servants eventually managed to revive her so that she was able to regain enough decorum to go see her son. When mother and son came together, they wailed so much that it sounded as if mourning for the deceased had begun all over again.

When Gildong finally managed to stop crying, he consoled her. "Mother, please do not be sad anymore."

He then addressed his older brother. "I came in disguise because I was afraid that if it became known that your younger brother has come, harm might come to this household."

The mourning son replied, "You are right." And so he allowed Gildong to maintain his appearance.

Gildong informed him, "I found a radiant mountain[114] for our father's gravesite. Will you trust me on this matter?"

The mourning son replied, "I will see the place before I decide."

The next day, Gildong took some of the family members up a rocky cliff, where he sat down and addressed them. "How about this place?"

The mourning son looked around and saw that the terrain was rough and full of sharply protruding peaks.

He criticized Gildong for choosing such an inappropriate site. "How could you be so ignorant as to think that this would make a good location for our parents' grave?"

Gildong pretended to be disappointed and replied, "Brother, I am saddened that you do not see this place for what it is. Allow me to display my power to you."

He picked up an iron hammer and shattered the rocks around them until the land became pristine and luminous. He then dug a hole of several *cheok* in the ground, which raised a red mist that reflected the starlight of the constellations of the dipper and the ox. A pair of white cranes appeared and flew away.

The mourning son took Gildong's hand and spoke to him. "How impressive you are, my wise brother. What better place can there be than this?"

Gildong feigned concern. "There is no better land than this in Joseon, but I know of another site that is ten times greater. The only problem is that it is very far away. What do you think, older brother?"

The mourning son replied, "I would follow you without hesitation even if the place you speak of is a thousand *ri* away."

Gildong spoke to him. "Indeed, hundreds of *ri* away, there is a site that is so auspicious that our family will produce kings, lords, generals, and ministers from generation to generation. So I bid you to take charge of our father's body and follow me to the place."

The next day, as they were about to depart with the deceased's body, Gildong went to the minister's wife and spoke to her. "It has been almost ten years since this lowborn son left his mother. I am loath to strain our relationship further by parting from her again. So I bid you to allow me to take her with me so that we can prepare the feast for Father's monumental tablet[115] and go through the funeral rites together. I believe that is the right thing to do."

The minister's wife gave him permission, and he took leave of her the same day. Gildong, his mother, and the mourning son left the house, escorting the deceased's body to Seogang, where Gildong's generals were waiting with a ship. They dismissed the household servants and guards who had come with them before they went aboard. The ship then headed out to the endless sea with its mast to the wind and went forth like a tempest toward a faraway destination.

Many days later, they came across tens of ships that had sailed out to meet Gildong, to greet him upon his safe return from his journey and to bring him food to eat. They escorted the ship with the deceased's body to an island, where countless soldiers took up the coffin and carried it forth. Gildong cast aside his monk's garb and put on funeral clothes before he led everyone up a mountain, to a place that was the most radiant of lands. The gravesite that was built there was as magnificent as a royal tomb, inspiring the amazed mourning son to praise all of its fine qualities. Gildong commanded his soldiers to finish preparing the site as he and his family went through the funeral rites until it was finally time to lower the coffin into the ground. The mourning son and Gildong wailed together as they offered up sacrifices. The majesty of the ceremony was without equal.

After the rituals were completed, Gildong led his mother and older brother down to his house, where Lady Bek and the concubines Jeong and Jo awaited them in a row at the court-yard. They greeted their mother-in-law and brother-in-law and offered them decorous condolences, commending them for the great care with which they had escorted the deceased's body to its final resting place. They then served them food and drinks. Chunseom knew not how to feel as she experienced both joy and sadness in the company of three such fair daughters-in-law. Then distinguished visitors arrived at the gate to offer their condolences, so that the grandness of the occasion knew no bounds.

After some time, the mourning son thought he should return to his own country, so he spoke to Gildong. "Since I have bur-ied my father here I do not wish to leave, but it pains me to stay when I know that the great wife[116] is waiting for me with an anxious heart."

As Gildong made arrangements for his brother's departure, the mourning son spoke again. "The mountains here are grand and the waters vast, but I feel such sadness from not knowing when we will see each other again." And his tears fell like rain.

Gildong consoled him. "Older brother, do not grieve so. Our father is buried in a radiant place so our family will produce kings, lords, ministers, and generals from one generation to the next, and no harm will come to you from the false charges of others. So I bid you to return safely to the great wife and con-sole her well. I also wish you a long and healthy life. I will make certain that proper rites are performed at our father's grave with the utmost care, as I look forward to the day when mother, son, and brothers will meet again."

The mourning son still felt a great sorrow from having to

leave. He bade farewell to everyone before he and Gildong took the ceremonial litter[117] carrying the monumental tablet of the deceased and returned to the gravesite. There, they wailed together in mourning once more before they went back down and loaded the litter onto a small ship.

The mourning son let out a sigh. "Our brotherhood, which is like the procession of wild geese,[118] is sundered north and south, so how sad I am."

As they bade farewell to each other by the ship, Gildong spoke. "Older brother, I wish you a comfortable journey through the many *ri* of your way home, and many years of health as you take care of the great wife. Please await my invitation to return here."

The mourning son replied, "Please find a way for me to visit our father's grave again."

They wept as they said their final farewells, the tears that filled their eyes flowing ceaselessly. A great deal of gold, silver, and silk was put on board before the ship was sent on its way.

After many days, the ship arrived at the mourning son's home country, where he went to the great wife and told her everything that had happened. He then wrote a letter to Gildong and gave it to the sailors before sending them on their way. The minister's wife praised all that she heard.

And so, on Jae Island, Gildong made certain that proper rites were performed at his father's gravesite, while Lady Bek and the concubines waited on their mother-in-law with great care. The land was at peace with no sign of trouble anywhere.

As time flowed on, Gildong slept on a straw mat and an earthen pillow until he completed the three-year mourning period. Upon his return to the world, he put on clothing of auspicious design and oversaw the improvement of agriculture and martial discipline in his realm. Eventually, the island's military strength became as mighty as a mountain, its weapons were stocked in abundance, and the people were ready to be mobilized.

There was an island country near Jae, and its name was Yul. Its land stretched out for tens of thousands of *ri*, and its provinces were managed by no less than twelve governors. It did not pay fealty to a greater country[119] and its rulers governed with benevolence from one generation to another, so the place was wealthy and its people lived in peace.

And so Gildong conceived a grand plan and worked to perfect it every day. The well-organized army under his command amounted to a hundred thousand cavalrymen and a hundred thousand foot soldiers.

One day, he summoned his generals and addressed them. "If we decide to overrun the world, there is no force that can stop us. We can remain on this small island of Jae, but then we may miss out on a great destiny Heaven has in store for us. I have heard that the country of Yul Island is wealthy and its strength is that of a powerful state. What do you warriors think?"

A general replied in agreement. "What you speak of has been the wish of my lifetime. How can a true man find contentment in growing old while leading a leisurely and mediocre life? I bid you to take command of our troops immediately and lead us to victory."

When Gildong saw that all were united in this purpose, he immediately set about raising his army. His placed his vice-general Mu Tong in charge of the advance guard, and organized the main body of his men into a formation composed of cavalry at the front and infantry in the rear. Gildong himself commanded the force in the center. On an auspicious day, he mobilized a powerful army of a hundred thousand. In the Year of the Blue Rat,[120] in the middle of the ninth lunar month, when the weather was warm and chrysanthemums were in full bloom, swords and spears were raised densely, and flags flew in a solemn manner. All of it resembled the military might of Ju Abu[121] of the state of Chu. Gildong led the army to a riverside, where men and supplies were loaded onto ships. They then put their masts to the wind and journeyed across the water.

When they arrived at their destination, they went forth with immense strength, the grand army sweeping across the land like an immense flood that no force could match.

The country of Yul Island had never experienced such a calamity before, so they could not resist the attack. Within months, Gildong accepted the surrender of about seventy castles, and he sent a letter to the King of Yul. The king's commander of gatekeepers brought the missive to the monarch, who opened it and read the following.

Hong Gildong, the leader of Hwalbindang from the Kingdom of Joseon, writes to the King of Yul.

It is a general truth that no one man holds an absolute right to rule over a country. As such, Seong Tang brought down Geol, and King Mu brought down Ju.[122] From ancient times, the subjugation of one's enemy has been regarded as a legitimate task for one to engage in, so I raised a righteous army and crossed the waters to find that none can rival our strength. With one beat of our drum, about seventy castles have surrendered in the face of our magnificence. So I bid the King of Yul to take stock of his own skills and come quickly to meet us in battle to decide our final victory or defeat. If you are afraid to do so, then open up your gates promptly and surrender. Willingly abdicate your throne, and I will not only spare your life but also see to it that generations of your ancestors are honored and that your progeny enjoy much wealth and respect. If you decide to go against the will of Heaven and resist my command, you will be defeated in battle and your country will fall with the burning of jade and rock alike.[123] You should consider this matter carefully.

The king could hardly contain his rage as he summoned his civil and military officials to consult with them. "An insignificant criminal has dared to act with such impudence. Who among you will swiftly capture this bandit and relieve the country of its worry?"

His officials replied, "If the great king should act out of momentary anger and risk everything by sending his troops out to fight, how embarrassing it would be to posterity if they were defeated. We should firmly close up the castle and not venture outside. Perhaps they will eventually leave on their own accord."

The king spoke out in anger. "The enemy army will soon reach this castle. How can we not fight back and just wait for them to depart?" So the king mobilized his soldiers and led them personally to the field.

A soldier came to him with urgent news. "The enemy army has already taken many castles, and it is heading here on three different roads."

The alarmed king hurriedly gathered his force and marched them to a place called Yanggwan, where he found the enemy already dug in at its sandy ground. The monarch set up his camp in the direction facing enemy headquarters and observed the formation of his opponent's force.

He laughed out loud and spoke. "How could I worry myself over such a mob?"

The next day, the king opened up the camp gates and went forth to provoke battle. Gildong put on dragon-scale armor and a golden helmet, took up his lance, and mounted a white horse with a bluish mane. He whipped the horse forward past his soldiers and loudly reprimanded the King of Yul. "Does the King of Yul not know of Hong Gildong of the Kingdom of Joseon? I received the command of Heaven and came here on a righteous cause. Yet you refuse to submit to fate and persist in resisting me. Stretch out your neck so that it may receive the blows of my sword."

The King of Yul was infuriated by those words, so he charged and gave battle to his opponent. The two armies fought forty rounds with no decisive result, until Mu Tong arrived with the soldiers under his command and joined the fight by enveloping the enemy. The noise of gongs and drums shook heaven and earth. The King of Yul took fright and turned his horse around to ride back to camp.

Suddenly, a violent wind arose and a dark mist filled the air in all directions so that the king could not find his way.

"King of Yul, do not run but surrender to me immediately," a voice said with force like thunder.

The King of Yul lamented to Heaven, "I meet my doom from underestimating my enemy, so I have no one to blame but myself."

He took up his sword and committed suicide. The entire country of Yul Island capitulated at once to Gildong, who led his men to the camp of his fallen enemy. He took the dead bodies of the King of Yul and his son[124] and gave them a royal funeral. The next day, Gildong gathered his three armies and entered the central castle of Yul Island, where he pacified the people and organized a congratulatory feast for his soldiers. He then granted various positions and titles to his generals, including Mu Tong, who was made a royal inspector tasked with touring the island to manage its populace.

On the first day of the twelfth lunar month of the year, Gildong made himself the king of the island and named his country Annam.[125] He appointed various people to government positions and invested the posthumous title of King Hyeondeok[126] upon his father and Queen Hyeondeok[127] upon the great wife. Gildong's own mother became the dowager queen, and his concubines Jeong and Jo were respectively entitled consort *chungryeol* of the left and consort *chungryeol* of the right,[128] while his father-in-law, Bek Yong, was made a grand lord of the court.[129] The gravesite of his father was named the Royal Tomb of Seol, where proper sacrifices were made and men were put on permanent guard. He then granted general amnesty to everyone on the island and had the royal palace thoroughly cleaned and washed. He finally sent envoys to Jae Island, to bring his family to him in a grand procession of the highest majesty. The dowager queen, the queen, and the two consorts all consoled him for the hardship he had gone through, and they greatly enjoyed one another's company.

After his ascendance to the throne, the new king ruled with such benevolence that his subjects drummed their full stomachs and sang happy ballads. "A time of peace and prosperity has come, like in the days of Yo and Sun."[130]

One day, the king made a pronouncement at the end of a morning meeting with his officials. "I originally came from the Kingdom of Joseon. My father, who now rests in the Royal Tomb of Seol, was a high minister in Joseon and I myself was the minister of war. I was granted three thousand *seok* of rice, which allowed me to move to Jae Island and achieve the great things that ultimately led to my attainment of kingship. How can I forget the favor I received from Joseon? My older brother is one of the most loyal subjects of his generation. So I am thinking of sending a memorial to the King of Joseon to express my gratitude, and to have someone pay respects at the graves of my ancestors. What is your opinion on this matter?"

His officials replied, "Your royal desire is most fitting."

The king was pleased as he addressed them. "Who among you will take on this task?"

His officials responded, "We believe that Jang Hoe, the royal secretary,[131] would make a capable emissary."

So the king made Jang Hoe his royal envoy and addressed him. "I command you to go to Joseon and deliver my memorial to the king, and then go to the graves of my ancestors and perform proper rites there. Afterward, bring Queen Hyeondeok and my older brother here. Should you complete the tasks well, I will reward you with an important position in the court."

Jang Hoe bowed down and replied, "I will do my utmost to escort them here with great care, so I bid Your Majesty to concern yourself no more about this matter." He then took leave of the king.

The emissary oversaw the collection of great gifts to Joseon and took charge of his sovereign's memorial to the Joseon court as well as his letters to Queen Hyeondeok and to his older brother. After a few days of preparation, he went to a riverside and boarded a ship that departed for Joseon. When it landed at Seogang in Joseon's capital, he went directly to the royal court and presented the memorial.

The King of Joseon had heard no word of Gildong for a long time, until one day the chief royal secretary came to him with the news that a memorial from the King of Annam had arrived. The surprised monarch quickly opened the letter and read the following.

"Your former minister of war, who is now the King of Annam, bows to you a hundred times as he sends this letter. Despite my low background, I have now become a monarch, all thanks to your grand benevolence. When I think of all that has passed, I am filled with awe at Your Majesty. I beg you not to refuse the gift of silver I am sending you. I wish you a long and healthy life. Long live Your Majesty."

After the king finished reading the memorial, he praised it with astonishment and joy. Jang Hoe prostrated himself before the monarch and spoke. "My king would like me to pay respects at his ancestors' graves in his stead, so I beg Your Majesty to give me leave to do so, and to write your response to my sovereign."

The king granted him permission and immediately summoned the minister of personnel Hong Inhyeon[132] and appointed him as the royal envoy of consolation and counsel[133] to the Kingdom of Annam.

He spoke to him. "Go with the emissary to the graves of your ancestors and pay your respects there."

Inhyeon expressed his gratitude and returned home, where he was visited by the emissary, who presented him with the letters sent by his king. The great wife and the minister of personnel read them with much praise. The next day, they went to the graves of the family's ancestors, where the emissary played his king's part in reading out the prayer to the dead and

offering sacrifices. After the completion of the rites, they returned to the court, where the King of Joseon complimented
them for properly fulfilling the rituals. Inhyeon took leave of
his sovereign with gratitude and then returned home to escort
his mother on their journey out of Gyeongseong. They all went
aboard the emissary's ship, which sailed forth and met a fa-
vorable wind. After a few months they reached Annam. The emissary sent ahead a written pronouncement of the arrival of Queen
Hyeondeok and the lord minister. The joyful king sent an envoy
to greet them and then raised Jang Hoe's position in the court. As
the honored visitors made their way to the capital, the emissary
notified every place of their coming, so they were greeted in each
town with a fanfare worthy of a royal procession.

When the king's envoy met them, he presented them with the
monarch's letter of welcome and announced Jang Hoe's promotion to his new position. Jang Hoe expressed gratitude for his
sovereign's favor and led the visitors on until they arrived at the
capital city a few days later. The king came out a hundred *ri* to
meet them and to escort them to his abode. Upon their arrival,
the monarch exchanged formal greetings with his guests, followed by the dowager queen, the queen, and the two consorts.
They then all sat down together. The great wife felt tremendous
joy from meeting them all and regarded the king with special
affection. The king opened the letter of consolation and counsel
from the King of Joseon and read the following.

> Because of my lack of benevolence, I missed the opportunity of
> having a great hero like you in my service. I know that you would
> have shown me great loyalty. Even now, when you have become
> a person of great importance, you have not forgotten me. Instead,
> you thought of our relationship of old and sent an emissary
> across the vast blue ocean to ask after me. How can I not be
> moved by such fidelity?

After the king finished reading, he came down from his
abode and bowed northward to express his gratitude.

Queen Hyeondeok asked a question. "Where is the tomb of the lord minister?" She wished to visit the place, so the king immediately picked a day for it.

He ordered Dol Tong, his state councilor of the left, to escort the great wife and the minister to the Royal Tomb of Seol on Jae Island. In accordance with the king's instructions, their traveling procession was organized in a majestic manner that was without rival in its grandeur. As they traveled through the roads from one town to the next, they were greeted and attended to with due magnificence. After many days, they arrived on Jae Island, where they were met by all of its officials, who escorted them to the Royal Tomb of Seol. There, the old minister's wife and the minister wailed in mourning before the grave, then read aloud a funeral address that they had composed for the deceased. Afterward, they looked around the area and saw that the place featured the fairest view, and they marveled at Gildong's wondrous talent in finding such a site. They sorrowfully bade their final farewell to the deceased before the tomb's stone table and came down to stay at the castle of the local district.

That night, the great wife had a dream in which the lord minister greeted her with joy and consoled her. It all seemed so real that she forgot that he was deceased and basked in the vision. After that night, she stayed in bed with health complaints, until she lost her consciousness for good. Her son took fright and nursed her to the best of his ability, but no medicine could revive her. So she passed away, at the age of seventy-eight. The minister grieved that he should suffer such an earth-shattering loss in a foreign land. He wailed until he could not breathe, so all those around him had to calm and console him until he regained his composure enough to send an emissary to the king, informing him of what had occurred.

At this time, the king sensed the flow of fortune and misfortune in the air and spoke out. "Queen Hyeondeok has passed away."

He then loosened his hair[134] and wept as he began his

mourning. He appointed an envoy to act as the organizer of funeral rites and instructed him to go and perform all the necessary rituals before burying the deceased at a designated spot on the left side of the Royal Tomb of Seol. The envoy was on his way to the gravesite when he met a messenger on the road who was coming to announce the death, and both of them marveled at how the king had known of it before word had arrived. After the envoy arrived on Jae Island, he expressed his condolences to the bereaved and saw to it that all the funeral rites were conducted with the utmost care. Within three months,[135] the body was interred at the Royal Tomb of Seol and the envoy escorted the minister to the capital city of Annam. Many days later, they arrived there and were met by the king, who grieved with his older brother and consoled him. The king then took him into his abode, where they joined his wives. And they all wailed together in great sadness at the final ceremony.

Time flowed on, and after the minister went through his three-year mourning period, he began to worry over the affairs of his sovereign and the state of his household in Joseon. When he asked his brother for leave to return to his home country, the monarch immediately organized a great feast so that they could enjoy themselves before his departure.

On the day of their parting they held each other as they wept and lamented. "How sad it is that this is the final parting of brothers who will never see each other again in this world."

And so they grieved over their separation.

The minister left the palace and sent word to Jae Island of his coming. The king accompanied him for a hundred *ri* and gave him a final farewell banquet with immeasurable sadness. The minister departed from the king and came to Jae Island, where he went to the Royal Tomb of Seol and mourned as he took his leave. He then bade farewell to all the officials of the land before he finally left for his country. He crossed the great sea and arrived in Gyeongseong, where he reported to the king before going home. There, he gathered his wife and children and told them all about what he had experienced, praising Gildong all the while.

After the King of Annam parted from his brother, he went back to the castle of his capital city. Time flowed on and Queen Chunseom reached the age of seventy. In the Year of the Red Snake,[136] in the middle of the ninth lunar month, she passed away. The king and his wives loosened their hair and wept as they began their mourning. Within three months, the deceased was interred on the right side of the Royal Tomb of Seol while the funeral rites were performed. The bereaved could hardly cease their wailing.

Through the benevolent rule of the king, the country was at peace and saw rich harvests, the people feeling secure with their households well stocked. No inauspicious incident disturbed the country. The king spent his days enjoying the performance of music. He saw the birth of three sons, the oldest of whom was given the name of Seon. He was the child of the queen. The second son was named Chang and was born of Consort Jeong, while the third, named Hyeong, was born of Consort Jo. The king designated his oldest son, Seon, as his crown prince; granted his second son, Chang, the title of lord of Jae Island; and his third son, Hyeong, the title of duke of Jae Island. He gave the lord of Jae Island the responsibility of overseeing the rites at the Royal Tomb of Seol and sent the mothers of his younger sons to live with them.

Thirty years after the king had ascended to the throne, he reached the age of sixty. One day, he was overcome by such sadness that he could not settle his mind. He wanted to follow the way of holy men,[137] so he summoned his officials and suddenly abdicated in favor of his heir. He then brought together his most loyal men from old times and granted them treasures before he enjoyed himself with music in their company.

After the performance, he spoke out in a half-drunken state. "When I think upon the world, I see that a human being is as insignificant as a single piece of grain on a vast ocean, and that a lifetime can pass in the blink of an eye. It is in the natural order of things that people who are taken high are brought down low, and those who become rich are made poor again, as if our lives are nothing more than pieces on a game board. So I wish nothing more than to have Angi Saeng and Jeok Songja[138] as my friends."

He was then overcome by a sorrow so powerful that he could not stop grieving, and all of his officials wept at his sadness. He ended the party and oversaw the ascendance of King Seon.

About ten *ri* from the capital city, there was a radiant mountain called Myeongsin. It was the most pleasant place of the fairest scenery featuring many peaks and valleys. On clear days, one could see holy spirits ride about on many-colored clouds. There, the king built a clean and well-constructed thatched hut of several *gan*,[139] and lived there with his queen. He practiced the way of holy men daily by adhering to the rules of enlightened beings. He drank in the force of the sun at daytime and of the moon at nighttime, while taking no food, until his mind became so powerful that his white hair turned black and he regained teeth that he had lost.

One day, luminous clouds of many colors enveloped Myeongsin Mountain, and thunder and lightning shook heaven and earth. The new king took fright at the phenomenon and took all of his officials up the mountain, only to find the place devoid of clouds and settled down in a tranquil state. The monarch went into his father's hut and saw that everything was in order, but his parents were nowhere to be found. The distraught king and his officials became astonished and afraid, but there was nothing that could be done. So they returned to the palace and sent out people in all directions in search of the former king and queen, but they could find no trace of them. The king wailed in sorrow and sent envoys to Jae Island to inform his relatives there of what had occurred. The lord and the duke of Jae Island grieved at the news along with their mothers and went to the capital city, where they loosened their hair to begin their mourning. The family conducted a funeral ceremony by the thatched hut, but without a body. The place was named the Royal Tomb of Hyeon, where their father continued to be honored.

When the lord and the duke of Jae Island returned home, everyone from the palace came out to greet them and to mourn endlessly with them.

Notes

In order to replicate the reading experience of *The Story of Hong Gildong* in the original language as much as possible, I have transliterated Korean words with no exact English equivalents (e.g., units of measurement like *ri* and *jang*). Their significances are fully explained in the notes below. I have also done the same thing for Chinese names and titles, transliterating them from Korean and identifying them in the notes. So the philosopher Kongzi (Confucius) is written in the Korean form as Gongja, the book *Zhouyi* (Book of Changes) as *Juyeok*, and the city of Nanjing as Namgyeong.

INTRODUCTION

1. On the universal figure of the heroic outlaw see Eric Hobsbawm, *Bandits* (New York: The New Press, 2000); Paul Kooistra, *Criminals as Heroes: Structure, Power, and Identity* (Bowling Green, Ohio: Bowling Green State University Popular Press, 1989); and Graham Seal, *The Outlaw Legend: A Cultural Tradition in Britain, America, and Australia* (Cambridge, England: Cambridge University Press, 1996).
2. http://en.wikipedia.org/wiki/Korean_names.
3. The Joseon dynasty was founded in 1392 by General Yi Seong-gye (King Taejo, r. 1392–1398), who ascended the throne after completing his coup d'état of the Goryeo Kingdom. The dynasty came to an end in 1897 when the penultimate Yi monarch Gojong (r. 1863–1907) changed the beleaguered nation's name

to Daehan Jaeguk (Empire of Korea) as part of his desperate and ultimately futile effort to strengthen it against foreign powers. The country lost its independence to Japan in 1910 with the forced abdication of Gojong's son Sujong, the last royal ruler of Korea.

4. Kim Taejun, *Joseon soseolsa* (Seoul: Doseo chulpan, 1989), 71–78. Kim published a new edition of the work in 1939, under the title *Jeungbo Joseon soseolsa* (Enlarged History of Joseon Fiction), in which he adjusted the more flamboyant language of the original to make the text more scholarly. For comparison see Kim Taejun, *Jeungbo Joseon soseolsa* (Seoul: Hangilsa, 1990), 81–91.

5. Yi Sik, *Gukyeok Taekdang jip* (Translated Works of Taekdang), vol. 6 (Seoul: Minjok munhwa chujinhoe, 1996), 236.

6. Lee Yoon Suk, "Hong Gildong jeon *jakja nonui ui gyebo*" (The genealogy of discussion on the authorship of *Hong Gildong jeon*), *Yeolsang gojeong yeongu* 36 (December 30, 2012): 381–414.

7. Yi Myeongseon, *Yi Myeongseon jeonjip* (Complete Works of Yi Myeongseon), vol. 3 (Seoul: Bogosa, 2007), 244. On recent research into identifying the first prose work to be written in *hangeul* see Lee Pok-kyu, "*Chogi gukmunsoseol ui jonjae yangsang*" (The mode of existence of early Korean novels), *Gukjeeomun* 21 (2000): 25–44.

8. There, the following is found: "There are tales of old times that are widely known from town to town, about people like So Daeseong, Jo Ung, Hong Gildong, and Jeon Uchi. Each of those books was written in the *eonmun* script and narrates the life story of a single character." Quoted in Lee Yoon Suk, "Hong Gildong jeon *wonbon hwakjeongeul wehan siron*" (Essay on the determination of the original text of *The Story of Hong Gildong*), *Tongbang hakji* 85 (January 1994): 247–85, 271.

9. For details on laws concerning the status of secondary children, see Martina Deuchler, "'Heaven Does Not Discriminate': A Study of Secondary Sons in Chosŏn Korea," *Journal of Korean Studies* 6 (1988–89): 121–63.

10. In addition to Deuchler, "Heaven Does Not Discriminate," see JaHyun Kim Haboush, *A Heritage of Kings* (New York: Columbia University Press, 1998), 94–95.

11. On the role of secondary sons and people of other secondary status in late-nineteenth-century Joseon, see Kyung Moon Hwang, *Beyond Birth: Social Status in the Emergence of Modern Korea* (Cambridge, MA: Harvard University Press, 2004).

12. See Hobsbawm, *Bandits*, 42–63.

A NOTE ON THE TRANSLATION

1. See Lee Yoon Suk, "Hong Gildong jeon *wonbon hwakjeongeul wehan siron*" (Essay on the determination of the original text of *The Story of Hong Gildong*), *Tongbang hakji* 85 (January 1994).
2. See Hŏ Kyun, "The Tale of Hong Kil-tong," trans. Marshall R. Pihl, Jr., *Korea Journal* (July 1, 1968): 4–21, and Peter H. Lee, *Anthology of Korean Literature: From Early Times to the Nineteenth Century* (Honolulu: University of Hawaii Press, 1981), 119–47. For another translation of the *gyeongpan* 30 version, see *Hong Kil-tong chon / The Story of Hong Gil dong* (Seoul: Baekam, 2000)—no translator is credited.

TRANSLATION

1. **King Seonjong:** Korean kings of the Joseon dynasty are generally referred to by their posthumous "temple names." When the fourteenth king of Joseon died in 1608, he was originally given the temple name of Seonjong, but it was changed to the slightly loftier Seongjo in 1616 by the order of his son Lord Gwanghae. It is highly unlikely, however, that the reference here is to that monarch, who was known by the name for only a few years. The *gyeongpan* and *wanpan* versions of *The Story of Hong Gildong* identify the king in the narrative as Sejong the Great (r. 1418–1450), while the Jo Jongeop 31/33 version refers to King Sejo (r. 1455–1468). "Seonjong" may be a mistake, but since imagined locales also appear, it is likely that the author made up the king to create a fictional time for the story. That also has the advantage of avoiding problems of anachronism since government institutions like the Military Training Agency (*hullyeon dogam*, see note 83) and the Office for Dispensing Benevolence (*seonhye-cheong*, see note 96), which are mentioned later in the narrative and other variants of the story, were created after the reigns of Sejong and Sejo.
2. **Jangan:** One of several names used during the Joseon dynasty for the capital city of the kingdom (today's Seoul). In the course of the story it is also referred to as Gyeongseong and Gyeongsa.
3. **mo:** A placeholder term used instead of the real name of a person or a place. The personal name of the minister is not given here as if to protect the identity of an actual person, to make the narrative seem as if it is a historical account about real people.

4. **high minister:** (*jaesang*) The word refers to someone who attained one of the three highest positions in the government at the State Council (*uijeongbu*): chief state councilor (*yeong uijeong*), state councilor of the left (*jwa uijeong*), and state councilor of the right (*u uijeong*). Whenever there were two positions of near equal ranks, they were differentiated by the terms "left" (*jwa*) and "right" (*u*), with the left higher than the right. The three councilors acted as the closest advisers to the king. Although the actual power wielded by the high ministers differed from one period to another, from the reign of one king to another, the status of *jaesang* always represented the apex of prestige in government service. Later in the narrative, it is mentioned that Minister Hong was once the *usang* (another name for state councilor of the right), the third-highest position in the state.

5. **assistant section chief:** (*jwarang*) The hierarchy of state service positions, attained after passing the *mungwa* civil service examinations (see introduction) and then through promotions, was organized into nine grades (*pum*), each of which was subdivided into the senior (*jeong*) and the junior (*jong*) for a total of eighteen ranks, with the highest rank of senior first (e.g., the *jaesang*, the high ministers of the State Council), and the lowest of junior ninth. Assistant section chief (*jwarang*) is a position of senior sixth rank.

6. **Ministry of Personnel:** The central bureaucracy of the Joseon government was composed of the Six Ministries (or Boards) of Personnel, Taxation, Rites, War, Punishments, and Public Works. The Ministry of Personnel (*ijo*), where Hong Inhyeon works, handled matters pertaining to appointments and promotions in state service.

7. *jang*: A unit for measuring length. Its value changed over time but through most of the Joseon dynasty period a *jang* measured a little over two meters (approximately 6.5 feet).

8. **great happiness in his heart:** Traditionally, a dream featuring a dragon is a sign of a great fortune to come. It was important, however, to keep the dream a secret until the fortune came about, since revealing it could negate the prophecy.

9. **inner chamber:** (*naedang*) Married couples of respectable *yangban* families slept and spent much of their time in separate quarters. The wife's chamber was known as *naedang* and the husband's *sarangbang* (outer chamber).

10. **he made her a concubine:** During the Joseon dynasty, a man could have only one woman as his wife (though polygamy had

been allowed previously, during the Goryeo dynasty), but men who could support more than one woman in their household brought extra women in as their concubines. See introduction.

11. **lunar months:** Prior to the modern era, the yearly calendar was reckoned by the twelve cycles of the moon (29–30 days), with the new year beginning with the appearance of a new moon, usually in late January or early February.

12. **hear only one thing to understand ten:** From "One who understands ten things from hearing only one thing," a traditional expression of admiration for a particularly intelligent and astute person. The saying is of ancient origin, an example of which can be found in *The Analects*, in a passage in which Kongzi (i.e., Confucius) asks his disciple Zi Gong about the intellectual capability of Yan Hui (Kongzi's favorite disciple). Zi Gong answers, "How dare I compare myself with Hui? Having learned one thing, he gives play to ten." (Book 5, 9) Confucius, *The Analects*, trans. Annping Chin (New York: Penguin Classics, 2014), 64.

13. **if he dared to call him Father:** "I cannot address my father as Father, my older brother as Brother"—the famous complaint of Hong Gildong that is repeated throughout the story. The expression encapsulates the frustrating condition of being a secondary child of a concubine with no legal standing in society.

14. **Gongja and Maengja:** Korean names for the Chinese philosophers Kongzi (Confucius—traditional dates, 551–479 BCE) and Mengzi (Mencius—traditional dates, 372–289 BCE), the founding thinkers of Confucianism.

15. **my portrait memorialized in Girin House:** An expression used to mean one has become renowned for having performed a great service for the country. *Giringak* (Girin House) is Korean for the Chinese *Qilinke*. *Qilin* is a mythological animal that was described as a combination variously of different parts of a dragon, a tiger, a deer, an ox, and a horse, sometimes with a horn. Later it was identified with the giraffe (*girin* is the word for a giraffe in modern Korean). In Chinese history, the Han dynasty emperor Wu (r. 141–87 BCE) built a garden in the capital city of Changan that was called Qilin Garden. His grandson, Emperor Xuan (r. 74–49 BCE), built Qilin House at the site, and in it he displayed the portraits of eleven of his most loyal and meritorious subjects in a hall of fame. Both the garden and the house were destroyed after the fall of the Han dynasty, but the fame of the building survived in the expression signifying the achievement of the highest recognition for service to the country.

16. **"Kings, lords, generals, and ministers are not made from a special blood":** An ancient expression of Chinese origin, from the writings of the grand historian Sima Qian (145–86 BCE), in his biography of the rebel Chen She. It means that anyone, no matter how humble his origin, can attain positions of power and prestige given the right set of circumstances, talents, and ambitions. It also implies that people who are already in positions of power are not there because of some innate quality of their inherited blood. Burton Watson, in his translation of Sima Qian, renders the expression as: "Kings and nobles, generals and ministers—such men are made, not born." See Sima Qian, *The Records of the Grand Historian: Qin Dynasty*, trans. Burton Watson (New York: Columbia University Press, 1993), 219.

17. **royal insignia:** (*byeongbu*) This was a special insignia granted by the king to a military commander of high status. A wooden panel inscribed with the royal order granting the general his rank and mission was split in two, and the commander carried one half while the other half remained in the capital with the monarch. The perfect fit of the two pieces guaranteed that the insignia was genuine.

18. **Jang Chung's son Gilsan:** Jang Gilsan was a real-life outlaw who operated during the reign of King Sukjong (r. 1661–1720). Originally an itinerant entertainer, an occupation of lowborn status (*cheonmin*), he became the bandit leader of landless peasants. He is also mentioned in *gyeongpan* versions of *The Story of Hong Gildong*. This reference poses one of many problems in attributing the authorship of the work to Heo Gyun, who died in 1618, decades before the appearance of Jang Gilsan. This also makes it problematic to identify the Hong Gildong of the story with the real-life bandit Hong Gildong who lived during the time of Lord Yeonsan (r. 1494–1506).

19. **the Way:** *Do* is the Korean word for the Chinese *dao*, the practice of which can denote mastering esoteric or supernatural knowledge, including the principles of Daoist philosophy, or learning some specialized skill, including a martial art.

20. **Mother Goksan:** Minister Hong's senior concubine, Chorang. Commoners and lowborn people were often referred to by the name of their hometown rather than their personal name. As revealed several paragraphs later, Chorang comes from the town of Goksan in Hwanghae Province. Although concubines had no legal standing in society, they were part of an informal hierarchy within the household. As she was the minister's senior concubine,

Gildong, the son of a junior concubine, was obligated to treat her with the respect due to a household "mother."

21. **courtesan:** (*gisaeng*) A professional entertainer and prostitute, a lowborn status (*cheonmin*) occupation for women, comparable to the Japanese geisha.

22. **Yi Taebaek and Du Mok:** Korean names for the Chinese figures Li Bai (701–762; courtesy name Li Taibai) and Du Mu (803–852), two of the greatest poets of the literary golden age of the Tang dynasty (618–907). They were famed throughout East Asia not only for their poetic skills but also for the nobility of their bearing.

23. **shamans and physiognomists:** (*munyeo* and *gwangsangnyeo*) Both were occupations of lowborn status (*cheonmin*), mostly for women (male shamans and physiognomists were rare, as they are in modern-day Korea). Shamans conjured sprits to bring fortune, to dispel misfortune, and to prognosticate the future, while physiognomists read people's facial features to tell their fortunes. For a fascinating study of the life of a contemporary shaman, see Laurel Kendall, *The Life and Hard Times of a Korean Shaman: Of Tales and the Telling of Tales* (Honolulu: University of Hawaii Press, 1988).

24. **Sungrye Gate:** During the Joseon dynasty, the capital city (alternatively referred to in this story as Jangan, Gyeongseong, Gyeongsa—today's Seoul) was protected by a wall all around it, with four great gates (*daemun*) at the four directions. An alternative name for the Great South Gate (*Namdaemun*) was Sungrye Gate. It is in today's Jung District of Seoul.

25. *nyang*: The Joseon dynasty currency. It is difficult to estimate its value, as it varied from period to period, but typically a *nyang* bought about five *mal* (around thirty liters or seven gallons) of rice in autumn, when the grain was plentiful after harvest season, and about two *mal* (around twelve liters or three gallons) in spring. Chorang's gift of fifty *nyang* is a substantial amount.

26. **the destruction of your entire family:** The Joseon dynasty punishment for treason, especially for those who sought to usurp the throne, was death not only for the perpetrator but also for three generations of his household (i.e., parents, siblings, and children), which effectively wiped out the entire family. The physiognomist is warning that since Gildong possesses the qualities of a king, he might harbor a royal ambition in the future and engage in actions that could cause the destruction of all the members of the family. It is interesting that while the physiognomist is

seeking to slander Gildong in order to turn his father against him, her discernment of his kingly nature turns out to be correct as he does become a monarch in the end.

27. **"Kings, lords, generals, and ministers are not made from a special blood":** The physiognomist repeats the Sima Qian quotation uttered previously by Gildong (see note 16), but with a different nuance. Gildong was lamenting his condition, wondering how Sima Qian could claim that anyone, no matter how humble his background, can rise to a position of power when his own status bars him from all legitimate paths to social advancement. In this case, however, the physiognomist is warning the minister that precisely because anyone can rise to power under the right set of talents and circumstances, Gildong might conceive the idea that he could do so himself, which could lead to the destruction of the family.

28. **the Six Teachings and the Three Summaries:** (Yukdo samryak), Korean for the Chinese Liutao sanlue, two classics of military strategy. The Six Teachings (Liutao) is attributed to Jiang Ziya, an adviser to King Wen, who founded the Zhou dynasty in 1046 BCE. The Three Summaries is associated with the Han dynasty general Zhang Liang (262–189 BCE), who is thought to have received it from a legendary figure named Huang Shigong. English translations of both texts can be found in The Seven Military Classics of Ancient China, trans. Ralph D. Sawyer (Boulder, CO: Westview Press, 1993), 40–105 and 292–306.

29. **astrology, geomancy:** The Korean words cheonmun and jiri can denote the modern scholarly fields of astronomy and geography, respectively, as well as the magical arts of astrology and geomancy (pungsu jiri). Later in the narrative, Gildong examines the stars to fathom the health of his father, who is far away, and uses his knowledge of land to pick out auspicious sites for his parents' tombs, so astrology and geomancy are the appropriate translations here. (For more on geomancy see note 113.)

30. **"What is said in daytime is overheard by the bird, and what is said in nighttime is overheard by the rat":** A traditional proverb meaning secrets are hard to keep because someone is bound to gossip and be overheard.

31. **Juyeok:** Korean name for the ancient Chinese classic of philosophical magic and divination, Zhouyi—better known in the West as I Ching or the Book of Changes.

32. **assistant section chief:** (jwarang, see note 5) To this day, Koreans commonly refer to one another by their professional positions even among close acquaintances. In the course of the story,

as Minister Hong's older son, Inhyeon, attains various different appointments throughout his career, he is referred to as the third minister (*chamui*), the governor of Gyeongsang Province (*Gyeongsang gamsa*), and the minister of personnel (*ipan*—short for *ijo panseo*).

33. **broken steamer:** The expression (*jeungi paui*) refers to a cooking implement made of earthenware, used for steaming food, that has been broken. It denotes a done deed that cannot be taken back, and so it is useless to regret it. Comparable in meaning to the English expression "spilled milk," as in "no use crying over spilled milk."

34. **the third or fourth watch:** In the Joseon dynasty, a day was divided into twelve units of roughly two hours each. The five units of nighttime were called *gyeong*, or "watches." The third and fourth watches, during which time Teukjae is to kill Gildong, roughly fall into, respectively, eleven o'clock at night to one, and one in the morning to three.

35. **He then unleashed his sorcery:** Gildong uses the magical Eight Trigrams found in the *Juyeok* (Chinese *Zhouyi*) to alter the directional orientation of the room, which confuses the intruder and subjects him to hallucinations.

36. *cheok*: A unit for measuring length. As with *jang*, its value changed over time, but a *cheok* is a tenth of a *jang*, and so was a little bit over twenty centimeters (approximately 0.65 feet) through most of the Joseon dynasty period.

37. **Supreme King of Cho:** Cho Paewang, Korean name for the Chinese ruler Chu Bawang, or Xichu Bawang (the Supreme King of Western Chu, the royal title of Xiang Yu, 232–202 BCE). O River is the Korean name for the Wu River in China, where Xichu Bawang committed suicide after most of his troops deserted him.

38. **Hyeong Gyeong:** Korean name for the Chinese scholar-warrior Jing Ke (unknown–227 BCE), who is famous for his failed attempt to assassinate King Zheng of the state of Qin (the future First Emperor of the Qin dynasty—Qin Shi Huang).

39. **The Silver River:** (*eunhasu*) Korean name for the Milky Way.

40. *ri*: A unit for measuring distance. Through most of the Joseon dynasty, a *ri* measured a little under 450 meters (just over a quarter of a mile).

41. **there must be a temple nearby:** Outside of cities, Buddhist temples tended to be built in remote areas to facilitate the monks' withdrawal from the world in environments conducive to meditation.

Many of them were located in high mountains and could be reached only after an arduous climb up rugged paths.

42. **Taesobaek Mountain:** A fictional mountain that combines the names of two actual mountain ranges in southern Korea, the Taebaek in North Gyeongsang Province and the Sobaek that splits off from the Taebaek to the southwest to stretch out between Gyeongsang and Jeolla Provinces.

43. **Gyeongseong:** One of several names for the capital city of Joseon (see note 2).

44. *geun*: A unit for measuring weight. One *geun* is about six hundred grams or 1.3 pounds.

45. **Haein Temple in Hapcheon County:** The most famous Buddhist temple in Korea, located in South Gyeongsang Province on Gaya Mountain. Built in the ninth century, it is one of the most important cultural sites in the country (designated a World Heritage Site by UNESCO in 1995). It houses the *Tripitaka Koreana*, the complete Buddhist scriptures carved into over eighty thousand individual wooden printing blocks.

46. *eum* and *yang*: Korean for the Chinese *yin* and *yang*, the two fundamental forces of the universe that represent the dark, the female, the low, and the cold on the one hand (*yin*), and the light, the male, the high, and the hot on the other (*yang*). To have studied and mastered the ways of *yin* and *yang* means to have gained an understanding of the essential workings of nature, possibly to the extent of knowing how to manipulate it at will. Hong Gildong possesses such a power of elemental magic.

47. **Sonja and Oja:** Korean names for the Chinese military theorists Sunzi (traditional dates, 544–496 BCE) and Wuzi (440–381 BCE). The former's treatise, better known in the West by the incorrectly translated title *The Art of War* (a better rendering of *Bing Fa* is "Military Rules"), is one of the major classics of Chinese military strategy. For English translations of the treatises of Sunzi and Wuzi, see Sawyer, trans., *The Seven Military Classics of Ancient China*, 157–86 and 206–24.

48. **three armies:** (*samgun*) A term meaning the entire military force of the country. After Yi Seonggye founded the Joseon dynasty in 1392, he formed the Three Armies Office (*uiheung samgunbu*, literally "Office of the Righteous and Flourishing Three Armies"), composed of his most loyal officers and soldiers, as the central military command of the kingdom. It played an important role in the stabilization of the new dynasty until it was reorganized under a different name in the mid-fifteenth century.

49. **Girin House:** See note 15.

50. **come to study:** Young men of *yangban* families often went to out-of-the-way places like Buddhist temples to concentrate on their studies before taking the civil service examinations. Even today many temples in isolated locales have facilities available for students studying for college entrance or other types of examinations.

51. **qualifying examination:** (*gyeongsi*) The first part of the civil examination one had to pass before one could move on to higher stages of the grueling literary examinations (*mungwa*).

52. **seok:** A unit for measuring volume. Traditionally, one *seok* was about 180 liters (around forty gallons).

53. **official announcement of the gift:** The announcement is sent to the government office in Hapcheon County to make the generous gift known to the public as a demonstration of noblesse oblige.

54. **name of Hwalbindang:** Hwalbindang is the famous name of Hong Gildong's group of bandits. In this text, the name is written in two alternative sets of Chinese characters, which give it slightly different meanings. The first two characters, *hwal* and *bin*, mean, respectively, "save" and "poor," and together they can mean "help the impoverished." The last character, *dang*, is signified in this instance by the character 堂, which denotes a location, a home, or a resting place. A few paragraphs down, however, *dang* is signified by the character 黨, which denotes an organized group of people, as in a faction or a league. So *Hwalbindang* could alternatively be understood as the name of the bandits' hidden village with the literal meaning of "the home of those who help the impoverished," or the name of the bandit group itself with the meaning of "a league of those who help the impoverished."

55. **eight provinces of Joseon:** Joseon was divided into eight provinces, each with an administrative center overseen by a governor who was appointed by the central government. The provinces were Pyeongan, Hamgyeong, and Hwanghae in the north; Gangwon and Gyeonggi (which contained the capital) in the center; and Chungcheong, Jeolla, and Gyeongsang in the south.

56. **money and grain being collected by the government:** Hong Gildong does not want to interrupt the regular and legitimate collection and dispersal of tax money and goods that are essential to the functioning of the kingdom.

57. **all members of Hwalbindang:** In this passage, Hwalbindang denotes "a league of men who dedicate themselves to helping the impoverished." (See note 54.)

58. **Hamgyeong Province:** Province in the northeastern part of the Korean peninsula.

59. **third watch:** (*gyeong,* see note 34) Roughly between eleven o'clock at night and one o'clock in the morning.

60. **royal tomb:** The administrative center of Hamgyeong Province was in the city of Hamheung, which was the hometown of Yi Seonggye, who founded the Joseon dynasty in 1392. The royal tomb is a reference to the gravesite of his ancestors, which was elevated to the status of a royal burial site after Yi's ascendance to the throne. Since one of the most important duties of the governor of Hamgyeong was to take care of the place, the idea of the site going up in flames would terrify him.

61. **"I will reward whoever catches Hong Gildong":** The sentence in the original translates literally as "I will reward whoever fails to catch Hong Gildong," which makes no sense, so it must be a textual error.

62. **gift treasures:** (*bongsong*) Gifts that provincial officials sent to influential people in the capital to curry favor with them. The sending of *bongsong* was regarded as part of an official's duty, but they often functioned as bribes paid for appointments to higher positions in the government, so Gildong sees them as legitimate targets.

63. **Supreme King of Cho:** The Chinese ruler Xichu Bawang (the Supreme King of Western Chu, the royal title of Xiang Yu, 232– 202 BCE). When Hong Gildong mentioned him previously (see note 37), he alluded to the king's tragic end, committing suicide on the shore of Wu River. Here, however, the reference is to the figure's renowned martial prowess and to the magnificence of his army.

64. **Jegal Gongmyeong:** Korean name for the legendary statesman, scholar, and military strategist Zhuge Kongming (Zhuge Liang, 181–234) of the Shu Han state. He is famous as the greatest military genius of his time and appears as a major character in the epic novel *The Three Kingdoms.*

65. **Palace of the Ten Kings:** In the Chinese Buddhist view of the afterlife (an amalgam of beliefs that developed from the seventh to the ninth centuries from Indian Buddhism and traditional Chinese mythology), the souls of the dead were taken to the Palace of the Ten Kings, where they were judged and punished for the acts of their lifetime by ten supernatural monarchs, before being sent on to be reincarnated in the living world. For details on the history and theology of the afterlife in Chinese Buddhism, see

Stephen F. Teiser, *The Scripture on the Ten Kings and the Making of Purgatory in Medieval Chinese Buddhism* (Honolulu: University of Hawaii Press, 1994).

66. **the Mansion of the Underworld, the Palace of the Ten Kings, and the House of Darkness:** (*jibu, sipjeon*, and *myeongbu*) Alternative names for the underworld of the afterlife.

67. **Bugak Mountain:** Mountain just north of the capital city. In today's Seoul, it is at the north end of the city center, above Gyeongbok Palace, the residence of the first Joseon dynasty kings.

68. **one-wheeled cart:** (*choheon*) A rickshaw on one wheel that held a high seat for a single rider. It was carried by four servants, two on either end, and was an official mode of transportation reserved for high-ranking government officials of junior second grade or above.

69. **two-horse litter:** (*ssanggyo*) A litter carried by two horses, one at the front and the other at the back. It was also reserved for people of high status.

70. **government inspector:** (*eosa*) Government inspectors were regularly dispatched to the provinces, where they sometimes traveled incognito to observe the implementation of state policy or to investigate corruption and incompetence on the part of local officials. In popular culture, they are often portrayed as heroic champions of justice, appearing deus ex machina at the end of a story to punish the wicked and to relieve the oppressed. The best example of this can be found in the ending of *The Story of Chunhyang*.

71. **state councilor of the right:** (*usang*, short for *u uijeong*) The third-highest position in the government below the king, a high minister position of senior first rank. (See note 4.)

72. **currently the third minister:** (*chamui*) A government position of senior third rank. Within an individual ministry, *chamui* was the third highest position, below that of minister (*panseo*) and deputy minister (*champan*). Since the time Gildong left home, his half brother, Inhyeon, has been promoted three grades (*pum*), or six ranks.

73. **Office for the Deliberation of Forbidden Affairs:** (*geumbu*, short for *uigeumbu*) A government office, directly overseen by the king, which investigated and meted out punishment for the most serious crimes, including treason.

74. **Injeong Hall:** The throne room at Changdeok Palace, which was built in 1412 as the second royal residence, after Gyeongbok Palace, in the newly established capital of the Joseon dynasty. Both palaces were destroyed during the Japanese invasion of 1592–98,

but Changdeok Palace was rebuilt in 1609, becoming the primary royal residence and governing center of the kingdom until 1872, when Gyeongbok Palace was rebuilt by order of the regent Lord Daewon.

75. **granted the third minister:** Hong Gildong's older brother, Hong Inhyeon, is now referred to as the third minister (*chamui*), his newly acquired position in the government.

76. **five relationships:** (*oryun*) One of the central concepts of Confucian philosophy, it refers to the five essential and sacred relationships that bind a society together. They were enumerated by the philosopher Mengzi—"love between father and son, duty between ruler and subject, distinction between husband and wife, precedence of the old over the young, and faith between friends" (Book III, Part A, 4). *Mencius*, trans. D. C. Lau (New York: Penguin Classics, 2005), 60.

77. **The governor:** Gildong's half brother, Inhyeon, is now referred to as the governor (*gamsa*, see note 32).

78. **Gyeongsa:** Another name for the capital city.

79. **cangues:** (*hangswae jokswae*) Implements for restraining dangerous or serious criminals. *Hangswae* denotes a large cangue, which consisted of two long wooden planks that were locked together around a prisoner's neck (with a hole large enough to fit around the neck but not wide enough to put one's head through). Because of its considerable size and weight it was extremely difficult to move around with. It was somewhat like the pillory, except that it was not fixed to a stationary base. *Jokswae* denotes a smaller version of the cangue, used to restrain the prisoner by the ankles.

80. **Office of the Royal Secretariat:** (*jeongwon*, short for *seungjeongwon*) A government office that dealt with sending commands from the king to the six ministries and receiving petitions from the ministries to the king. The royal secretaries of the office organized, formalized, composed, and advised the king on communications with the ministries.

81. **minister of war:** (*byeongjo panseo*) The head of one of the six central ministries of the government.

82. **disaster from falling upon three generations of your family:** Another reference to the penalty for treason.

83. **Military Training Agency:** (*dogam*, short for *hullyeon dogam*) In 1593, in the midst of the great crisis of the Japanese invasion (1592–98), this military institution was created as the defense force of the capital city. With a standing army of professional

soldiers, the agency was responsible not only for guarding the capital but also for training soldiers and developing new weapons (including improved firearms) and equipment. It functioned as the main defensive force of the central government until it was disbanded by King Gojong in 1882.

84. **Minister Hong:** Reference to Gildong himself, now that he has been made minister of war by the king.

85. **Namgyeong:** Korean name for the Chinese city Nanjing.

86. **Yul:** A fictional island.

87. **Yangcheon:** Name of a town outside the capital city, upstream on the Han River.

88. **Seogang:** Literally "West River," an area of the capital city on the northwestern side of the Han River. In today's Seoul, it falls under Mapo District.

89. **unhulled rice:** (*jeongjo*) Rice with its husk intact. Unhulled rice can be kept for a longer period before being eaten or planted. Gildong asks specifically for it because he needs to transport it all the way to his new home.

90. **eunuchs:** Eunuchs served as both the king's personal secretaries and servants in the Joseon dynasty. Employing eunuchs assured that no sexual activity would occur between them and the women living and working in the royal palace.

91. **the *Six Teachings* and the *Three Summaries*:** See note 28.

92. **the *Four Books*, the *Five Classics*:** The essential ancient Chinese texts that every educated man was expected to familiarize himself with (crucial for the literary civil service examinations). The *Four Books* are the four canonical works of Confucian philosophy—the three texts of Kongzi's sayings (*The Analects*, the *Great Learning*, the *Doctrine of the Mean*) and the text of Mengzi's sayings. The *Five Classics*, edited by Kongzi himself, were essential educational works of philosophy, literature, magic, and history: the *Classic of Poetry*, the *Classic of History*, the *Classic of Rites*, the *Classic of Changes* (*Zhouyi*, or *I Ching*), and the *Spring and Autumn Annals*.

93. **Office of Special Councilors:** (*okdang*) Informal name for *hongmungwan*. A government office responsible for advancing the study of Confucian philosophy, maintaining the Royal Library, and advising the king on matters pertaining to proper and righteous policies in governing. The three high ministers of the State Council (see note 4) oversaw the operation of the office as its highest-ranking members, so this was one of the most prestigious state institutions an official could work in.

94. **Yong Bong and Bigan:** Korean names for Long Feng and Bigan, two ancient Chinese historical figures who were renowned for their righteous service to their sovereigns. Guan Long Feng was chief councilor to King Jie (1728–1675 BCE), the cruel and dissolute ruler of the Xia dynasty, which fell under his mismanagement. Long Feng warned his monarch that his misrule would bring about the destruction of the country and was executed for his honesty. Bigan (a.k.a. Cai Shen) was the uncle of Emperor Di Xin (r. 1075–1046 BCE), also a cruel and dissolute ruler who brought about the fall of the Shang dynasty. Like Long Feng, Bigan warned his nephew of the consequences of his misrule and was executed for it. It is interesting that of all the historical figures famous for their righteous loyalty, Gildong names two who served under tyrannical, dynasty-losing monarchs and who were killed after courageously admonishing their sovereigns for their misbehavior.

95. **Your Majesty might take fright:** Because the king might also see the qualities of a monarch in Hong Gildong's eyes that the physiognomist saw.

96. **Office for Dispensing Benevolence:** (*seonhyecheong*) After the disaster of the Japanese invasion of 1592–98, the Daedong ("great unified") Law was promulgated in 1608 to bring relief to the still suffering populace. It was a uniform tax code that replaced the previous indirect tribute system, which was easily and often abused by corrupt landlords and tax collectors who took arbitrary amounts from the common people. As part of the implementation of the new law, the Office for Dispensing Benevolence was established as the primary tax-collecting agency. Taxes could be paid with money or items like rice, cloth, and artisanal products. The office, therefore, was in possession of hoards of goods in its warehouses, including a great many sacks of rice.

97. **Lord Neunghyeon:** Literally "a capable and intelligent lord," a fake princely title.

98. **Jae:** A fictional island.

99. **Mangdang Mountain:** Mountain in Fujian Province, China (Mangdangshan).

100. **a drug to use on an arrowhead:** Poison to make the arrow a more deadly weapon.

101. **Nakcheon:** Korean name for Luochuan, a county in China.

102. **the *Classic of Poetry*, the *Classic of History*:** Two of the *Five Classics*—ancient texts, edited by Kongzi, that educated people were expected to familiarize themselves with. (See note 92.)

103. **Du Mokji and . . . Yi Jeokseon:** Korean names for the Chinese poets Du Muzhi and Li Zhexian. The Tang dynasty literary figures were mentioned before (see note 22) in reference to Gildong's talents and noble bearing. Here, they are referred to by their honorific titles. Muzhi is Du Mu's courtesy name (given to men of respectable families upon reaching adulthood), and Zhexian is one of Li Bai's many honorific titles, meaning "immortal in exile" (i.e., "an immortal spirit who is temporarily dwelling in the world of humans").

104. **phoenix:** (*bonghwang*) One of the symbolic significances of the mythological bird (Chinese: *fenghuang*) was the coming together of the sexes, so the "union of the phoenix" denoted marital bliss, including the sexual relationship between husband and wife. The creature figures prominently in traditional Chinese and Korean wedding decorations.

105. **Hwa Ta and Pyeon Jak:** Korean names for the ancient Chinese physicians Hua Tuo and Bian Que. Hua Tuo (c. 145–208) was famous as a surgeon and is reputed to be the first to use anesthesia in his operations. The even more ancient and probably legendary Bian Que (c. 700 BCE) is the earliest recorded physician in Chinese history.

106. **Lady Bek:** Bek *sojeo*, Gildong's wife, daughter of Bek Yong.

107. **ja:** A unit for measuring length, same as *cheok* (see note 36).

108. **assistant section chief:** The last time Gildong's half brother, Inhyeon, appeared in the story, he was a third minister (*chamui*—rank of senior third grade) and then appointed as the governor of Gyeongsang Province by the king. Here he is referred to as an assistant section chief (*jwarang*—rank of senior sixth grade) again, which was his position when Gildong first left the Hong household. So either this is a mistake in the text or it means that he was demoted six grades since Gildong's departure from Joseon—perhaps as punishment for his relationship to Gildong.

109. **the Land of Yellow Spring:** (*hwangcheon*) A name for the land of the afterlife.

110. **mourning period:** The *yangban* families of the Joseon dynasty adhered to strict rules of mourning based on Neo-Confucian principles. When a man died, his son had to enter into a mourning period of three years (in actuality twenty-seven months with technical adjustment of the lunar calendar), during which he had to withdraw completely from social life (including relations with his wife and the company of other women), living simply in a

small hut built next to the gravesite and wearing coarse clothing. For detailed descriptions of mourning rites and their history, see Martina Deuchler, *The Confucian Transformation of Korea: A Study of Society and Ideology* (Cambridge, MA: Harvard University Press, 1992), 179–96, especially the useful chart on page 183 that shows different "mourning grades."

111. **monumental tablet:** (*yeongwi*) A wood panel with the name of the deceased written on it was displayed prominently during funerals. It was treated as if it contained the soul of the dead, so people mourned and paid their respects toward it. After the ceremony, it was taken home to be used during special occasions for the family to remember the deceased. Wealthy and respectable people living in a large household compound had a special room where monumental tablets were permanently displayed.

112. **mourning son:** (*sangin*) During the mourning period, Minister Hong's older son is referred to as *sangin* since he is the organizer and leader of funeral rituals. Although every child of the deceased, including an illegitimate one like Gildong, was technically a *sangin*, secondary children were not allowed to lead funerals of their parents during most of the Joseon dynasty.

113. **geomancy:** (*jiri*, short for *pungsu jiri*) By the time of the Joseon dynasty, the central task of this ancient art of geographical and environmental magic was locating auspicious lands (*myeongdang*: literally "radiant places") for the burial of the deceased. It was thought that laying one's parents to rest in such a place brought fortune to the living members of the family, while placing them in an inauspicious place brought misfortune. Geomantic treatises gave instructions on how to identify such locales. For more information on Korean geomancy see Deuchler, *The Confucian Transformation of Korea*, 197–202; Hong-Key Yoon, *The Culture of Fengshui in Korea: An Exploration of East Asian Geomancy* (Lanham, MD: Lexington Books, 2006); and Sun Joo Kim, *Marginality and Subversion in Korea: The Hong Kyŏngnae Rebellion of 1812* (Seattle: University of Washington Press, 2007), 89–98.

114. **radiant mountain:** (*myeongsan*) A geomantically auspicious mountain.

115. **feast for Father's monumental tablet:** In a respectable household, a deceased parent was regularly honored with a feast presented before the monumental tablet.

116. **great wife:** (*daebuin*) Honorific title given to the widow of an important personage.

117. **ceremonial litter:** (*yoyeo*) A litter is a platform that is carried by people, usually with a sedan chair for a highborn person to ride on, but a *yoyeo* is a specific type of litter that carries the monumental tablet of the deceased for a ceremonial purpose.

118. **wild geese:** The coordinated movement of wild geese in flight was used as a metaphor for the harmonious relationship of siblings.

119. **fealty to a greater country:** Korea paid fealty to various Chinese dynasties throughout its history. When Joseon was founded in 1392, it agreed to an "older brother–younger brother" relationship with Ming dynasty China. With the rise of the Qing (Manchu) dynasty in the mid-seventeenth century, Joseon, in the reign of King Injo, first resisted but finally capitulated to the new rulers of China in 1636. After Qing's defeat in the First Sino-Japanese War (1894–95) and its loss of influence in Korea, King Gojong declared an end to Joseon's tributary relationship with China by proclaiming the Empire of Korea (Daehan Jaeguk) in 1897.

120. **Year of the Blue Rat:** (*gapja*) In premodern Korea, years were reckoned through a sixty-cycle (sexagenary) system, the terms of which were created by matching one of five stems represented by the five basic elements and their associated colors—wood (blue), fire (red), earth (yellow), metal (white), and water (black)—to one of twelve branches denoted by the twelve astrological animals of rat, ox, tiger, rabbit, dragon, snake, horse, sheep, monkey, fowl, dog, and pig, for a total of sixty possible terms. The year of *gapja* is the first of the sixty-year cycle.

121. **Ju Abu:** Korean name for the Chinese historical figure Zhou Yafu (mid-second century BCE), a famed general of the Han dynasty (the text wrongly associates him with the state of Chu) renowned for the military discipline of his army. His greatest achievement was putting down the Rebellion of the Seven States (154 BCE) on behalf of the Han emperor.

122. **Seong Tang brought down Geol, and King Mu brought down Ju:** Reference to two Chinese rulers who established new dynasties by destroying previous ones. Gildong is telling the King of Yul that the rise and fall of these dynasties were natural to the flow of history, so he should resign himself to his inevitable fall and surrender to him. Seong Tang is the Korean name for the Chinese ruler Shang Tang (King Cheng Tang, the founder of the Shang dynasty, r. 1673–1646 BCE), and Geol is the Korean name for Jie, the tyrannical last monarch of the Xia dynasty (see note 94). King Mu is the Korean name for King Wu (the founder of the

Zhou dynasty, r. 1046–1043 BCE), and Ju is the Korean name for Zhou, the posthumous name of Di Xin, the tyrannical last monarch of the Shang dynasty. It is interesting that Gildong previously told the King of Joseon that he would have liked to have served him with the loyalty of Yong Bong (Long Feng) and Bigan, who were the subjects of the doomed kings Jie and Zhou mentioned here. So Gildong, who once aspired to the ideal of a loyal and courageous servant of his sovereign, has now taken on the role of a ruler who brings down a king and his dynasty.

123. **the burning of jade and rock alike:** An expression signifying the destruction of every person, high or low, righteous or wicked.

124. **the King of Yul and his son:** There was no previous mention of a son of the King of Yul who died, so there is probably a passage missing in this version of the story. The *gyeongpan* 30 text does tell of the crown prince and the Queen of Yul Island who followed the monarch in committing suicide after his defeat in battle.

125. **Annam:** *Annam* literally means "peaceful south," so "the Country of Annam" (*Annamguk*) could be rendered as "Peaceful Country of the South." Annam was also the southernmost province of China, which encompassed the northern part of Vietnam until the tenth century, and Vietnam as a whole was commonly referred to as Annam for much of the country's premodern history. In the imagination of the people of North Asia, however, the name evoked a legendary place in the general area of the exotic far south, so it should not be identified with any specific locale.

126. **Hyeondeok:** A royal title that literally means "manifestation of virtue." Dynastic founders posthumously granted such royal titles to their fathers.

127. **Queen Hyeondeok:** Technically, "queen to King Hyeondeok."

128. **consort *chungryeol* of the left and consort *chungryeol* of the right:** *Chungryeol* literally means "ardent fidelity." Two courtly positions of near-equal rank were differentiated by the terms "left" (*jwa*) and "right" (*u*), with the left higher than the right. So Jeong is made a consort of more senior status than Jo.

129. **grand lord:** (*buwongun*) The highest noble title granted to a meritorious subject, including the king's father-in-law.

130. **Yo and Sun:** Korean names for the legendary ancient Chinese rulers Yao (traditionally c. 24th–23rd centuries BCE) and Shun (traditionally c. 23rd–22nd centuries BCE), two of the semimythical Three Sovereigns and Five Emperors of the earliest period of Chinese history, who were revered by Kongzi and countless

others throughout the centuries as ideal monarchs under whose rule their realms enjoyed perfect peace and harmony. In *The Analects*, Kongzi says, "Sublime was the way Shun and Yu held possession of the empire" (Book 8, 18) and "Great was Yao as a ruler!" (Book 8, 19). Confucius, *The Analects*, 125–26.

131. **royal secretary:** (*hanrim haksa*) A special honorific title given to meritorious secretaries of the royal court.

132. **minister of personnel:** Gildong's half brother, Inhyeon, has attained the position of minister of personnel, a rank of senior second grade.

133. **royal envoy of consolation and counsel:** (*wiyusa*) This title for a royal envoy was usually given to a king's representative who was sent out to organize and dispense aid and resources in disaster-stricken places. See Anders Karlsson, "Royal Compassion and Disaster Relief in Chosŏn Korea," *Seoul Journal of Korean Studies* 20, 1 (June 2007): 71–98.

134. **loosened his hair:** In normal times, both men and women of *yangban* families kept their hair meticulously organized to maintain a respectable appearance. The men let their hair grow out, tying it in a topknot and keeping everything in order with the aid of headbands made of horsehair. With the commencement of the mourning period, however, the hair was loosened and allowed to hang free as a sign of both grief and the mourner's required withdrawal from society.

135. **Within three months:** In traditional funeral arrangements, careful consideration had to be given to the time of burial, as interring the body on an inauspicious date could bring misfortune to the descendants of the deceased. Due to the complex rules of ritualistic taboo, determining a good day for the burial could be a difficult task that took some time. During most of the Joseon dynasty period, high-status people were given up to three months for the purpose. See Deuchler, *The Confucian Transformation of Korea*, 198–99.

136. **Year of the Red Snake:** (*jeongsa*, see note 120) The significance of the year is unclear since it makes no sense when taken literally. The Red Snake year comes fifty-three years after the Blue Rat year, which is when Gildong invaded Yul Island. If his mother dies in the Red Snake year at the age of seventy, then she was seventeen when her son set off on the invasion. But she was nineteen when Gildong was conceived. Such references to years were probably made to mimic historical writings.

137. **follow the way of holy men:** A common theme in the legends of Daoist holy men is their withdrawal from society to isolate

themselves in remote locales (usually high mountains) to medi-
tate. Once they reach an essential understanding of the way of
the universe, they transcend themselves to a state in which they
become immortal, supernaturally powerful, and supremely indif-
ferent to the concerns of the world.

138. **Angi Saeng and Jeok Songja:** Korean names for the mythic Chinese holy men Anqi Sheng and Chi Songzi. They are two
famous examples of Daoist immortals (*xin*) who attained ever-
lasting life and supernatural power through the attainment of
ultimate wisdom. When Gildong says that he wants to become
friends with them, he means that he would also like to go into
isolation to study the way of the universe, in the hope of attain-
ing spiritual transcendence.

139. *gan:* A unit for measuring area. A *gan* is a little over 3.3 square
meters or thirty-five square feet.

THE STORY OF PENGUIN CLASSICS

Before 1946 . . . "Classics" are mainly the domain of academics and students; readable editions for everyone else are almost unheard of. This all changes when a little-known classicist, E. V. Rieu, presents Penguin founder Allen Lane with the translation of Homer's *Odyssey* that he has been working on in his spare time.

1946 Penguin Classics debuts with *The Odyssey*, which promptly sells three million copies. Suddenly, classics are no longer for the privileged few.

1950s Rieu, now series editor, turns to professional writers for the best modern, readable translations, including Dorothy L. Sayers's *Inferno* and Robert Graves's unexpurgated *Twelve Caesars*.

1960s The Classics are given the distinctive black covers that have remained a constant throughout the life of the series. Rieu retires in 1964, hailing the Penguin Classics list as "the greatest educative force of the twentieth century."

1970s A new generation of translators swells the Penguin Classics ranks, introducing readers of English to classics of world literature from more than twenty languages. The list grows to encompass more history, philosophy, science, religion, and politics.

1980s The Penguin American Library launches with titles such as *Uncle Tom's Cabin* and joins forces with Penguin Classics to provide the most comprehensive library of world literature available from any paperback publisher.

1990s The launch of Penguin Audiobooks brings the classics to a listening audience for the first time, and in 1999 the worldwide launch of the Penguin Classics Web site extends their reach to the global online community.

The 21st Century Penguin Classics are completely redesigned for the first time in nearly twenty years. This world-famous series now consists of more than 1,300 titles, making the widest range of the best books ever written available to millions—and constantly redefining what makes a "classic."

The Odyssey continues . . .

The best books ever written

PENGUIN CLASSICS

SINCE 1946

Find out more at www.penguinclassics.com